# LOVE CAN

Salvia told Monsieur Girard that she was tired.

"I really have no wish to dance anymore," she said firmly.

He paid the bill for their dinner.

Then they drove back in his carriage.

When she reached the hotel, she realised that it was not particularly late in the evening and maybe she had been rather rude.

She therefore did not over-protest when he insisted on going up to her sitting room to have, as he said, 'a last drink.'

Lord Carville had left a bottle of white wine on the sideboard.

She poured Monsieur Girard out a glass and then said,

"Now you must let me retire to bed, as I have told you I am feeling very tired."

He took the wine glass from her hand and put it down.

Then he said,

"That is exactly what I am thinking we should do."

Almost before she realised what was happening, he pushed her through the door beside them.

It was open and so he realised that it led into her bedroom.

Copyright © 2017 by Cartland Promotions

First published on the internet in August 2017

by Barbaracartland.com Ltd.

ISBN 978-1-78213-988-1

*The characters and situations in this book are entirely imaginary and bear no relation to any real person or actual happening.*

This book is sold subject to the condition that it shall not, by way of trade or otherwise, be lent, resold, hired out or otherwise circulated without the publisher's prior consent.

No part of this publication may be reproduced or transmitted in any form or by any means, electronically or mechanically, including photocopying, recording or any information storage or retrieval, without the prior permission in writing from the publisher.

# LOVE CANNOT FAIL

# BARBARA CARTLAND

Barbaracartland.com Ltd

*"I adore hearing other people's stories about love. How they fell in love, how love changed their lives and how they found each other in the most unlikely circumstances as if by chance.*

*But was it chance or was it destiny that was always going to happen as love is the most powerful force in the Universe and always will be?"*

Barbara Cartland

# CHAPTER ONE
# 1867

The Countess of Wenlock came down to breakfast rather late.

She always insisted on having breakfast downstairs rather than in her bedroom which most of her friends asked for after being out late the night before.

The Countess, however, was keen to keep herself active. It was only when she was in London entertaining and being entertained that she found it at all difficult to get up early in the morning.

It was nearly ten o'clock. which was pretty late for her. and breakfast was ready waiting for her in the dining room.

She sat down at the table and the butler put in front of her the scrambled eggs and bacon she enjoyed so much for breakfast.

She always had them whether she was in London or in the country.

The house in London was her favourite because it was so spectacular.

It had been built nearly two hundred years ago in the middle of London opposite what was now called Hyde Park and it stood back from the road which was known as Park Lane.

It had a large garden filled with shrubs flowers and many different vegetables just as it was at their house in the country.

She noticed, however, that to the North of her there were now houses facing onto Park Lane.

She was very afraid that one day they would extend further and stand in front of the house which had been in the Wenlock family ever since it was first built at least two centuries ago.

When her husband had died two years ago and her son became the Earl in his father's place, she was worried that he might get married and want her to leave their house in London if not the one in the country.

But Donald showed no sign of getting married.

He was merely enjoying himself speeding from one beautiful woman to another.

The Countess was very proud of her son and she was well aware that he was exceedingly good-looking with the result that women pursued him relentlessly.

For him it was inevitable that he went from one entrancing blossom to another.

Her daughter, the lovely Salvia, however, was very different.

She enjoyed the parties which, when she came to London, were waiting for her every night if she wanted to go to them.

But she really much preferred being in the country and riding the many excellent horses that her father had filled his stables with.

She had missed her father more than anyone else because he had found her so intelligent that he preferred to take her with him on his travels rather than his son.

There was only a year between them, but it always seemed to him that Salvia was the eldest simply because her intelligence and brain was much the same as his.

Before he had married he had travelled a great deal, but he found when Salvia grew older that it was easier to take her with him on his trips rather than her mother or his son.

"If I am not at home," her mother had said to him, "you know perfectly well the garden will not be properly looked after and our many horses and dogs might easily be neglected."

She had smiled at her husband as she added,

"Quite frankly, darling, I want to keep the house perfect for when you return from what I am grateful to say is seldom a very long voyage."

Actually he was engaged in running messages from Queen Victoria to other countries in Europe and the Middle East.

Because he was so astute it did not take him long to deliver them and to receive an answer that usually pleased Her Majesty.

Salvia always adored travelling with her father.

Although no one ever said so, it was perhaps she who missed him more than anyone else.

It was with some reluctance that the Countess came to London after he died when she would have much rather stayed in their country house.

At the same time she loved her London home and thought it was very good for Salvia to accept the many invitations that she had received from the very moment she became a *debutante*.

She was very pretty as well as bright and it seemed to quite a number of people that it was extraordinary she had not already been marched up the aisle with one of the handsome and grand gentlemen who had fought to dance with her.

Salvia had received several proposals of marriage, but she had no wish to leave home.

Compared to her father she found that the majority of young gentlemen she danced with were not particularly intelligent, however flattering they might be to her.

Looking round the breakfast room now and the sun outside the windows, the Countess thought that the flowers were particularly lovely.

'I do hate London when it's cold and frosty,' she thought to herself. 'But when the sun is shining, I love to be in the country.'

Then she laughed at herself for wanting too much when she already had a great deal to be thankful for.

She had just finished breakfast when Salvia came in wearing her riding clothes.

"I have just been in Rotten Row, Mama," she began. "You have never seen such a lot of stupid girls who want to ride because it is the vogue, but who have no idea how to handle a horse."

"I would suppose that they were admiring Bruno," her mother asked, knowing which horse she would have been riding this morning.

"All the men did," Salvia replied, "but the women were so busy trying not to fall off their saddles that they had no interest in anything but themselves."

The Countess laughed.

"You are not to be so critical, my darling, just because you ride divinely and no one could purchase better horses than your father."

"That is true," Salvia sighed.

She was just about to leave her mother when her brother came into the room.

"Oh, there you are, Donald," the Countess greeted him. "I heard that you had gone out."

"I went out early and I have come back to tell you I am afraid, Mama, that there is very bad news."

"Bad news?" the Countess questioned. "Why?"

"Because you will be angry with me when I tell you and I cannot believe that it has actually happened."

He was an extremely good-looking young man, but at twenty-five he still appeared, in some ways, more of a boy than a man.

He sat down, not at the end of the table where his father had always sat but near to his mother.

Then he said in a voice he could hardly recognise as his own,

"I really don't know how to tell you. Mama what has occurred."

His sister, who had been about to leave the room, came back and sat down at the other side of the table.

She did not say a single word, she only looked at her brother wondering what could have upset him so much and made him look so different from his usual happy and contended self.

There was a pause and the Countess urged him,

"Come along, darling, tell me what is wrong. I am certain that it cannot be as bad as you are anticipating it to be."

"It is worse," Donald answered glumly.

There was more silence before he began,

"You will remember that I mentioned the American who was here last week, who made himself very pleasant to me. In fact I enjoyed his company a great deal."

"Yes, you told me about him," the Countess said. "But I don't recall meeting any of his friends."

"I think that this was Walter's first visit to England and he told me that his family was one of the richest in New York, but none of them had ever been on a visit to England."

Donald was taking rather a long time over what he was saying.

Salvia was wondering if she should go and change her clothes, which she intended to do because she had an appointment later in the morning.

Then the Countess asked Donald,

"What has happened to your friend? Has he injured himself in any way?"

There was another pause.

And then Donald replied,

"He has gone back to America and taken all our money with him!"

There was a stunned silence and then the Countess asked him,

"What do you mean, Donald? I don't understand. How could he have taken our money?"

"He told me that as he was so rich he wanted to make me rich too. He told me that many of the things we had invested in here in England were very feeble compared to what they would pay in America for exactly the same projects."

He stopped and Salvia prompted him,

"Go on, Donald. What has happened?"

"I listened to everything that he told me and finally, I agreed to let him invest some of our money in New York, which he promised me would be magnified more than a thousand times."

Again there was silence until the Countess asked,

"I suppose you have a list of what he has taken."

"I cannot bear to tell you what has happened."

"But we have to know, of course we just have to know," Salvia exclaimed at once. "After all it is our money as well and we are entitled to know exactly where it has gone."

Donald drew in his breath.

"Very well. Walter has left England this morning taking every penny we possess with him!"

Salvia and their mother stared at him.

"What are you saying?" the Countess quizzed him. "How can he have taken all our money?"

"I can hardly believe that it is true," Donald replied. "But yesterday he asked me if he could see our books and what our money was invested in."

He coughed before he continued,

"I showed them all to him and, as I wanted to play tennis at the Club with Horace, who was supposed to be so good, I said to Walter, 'you can go through the books and take out the ones you think would be of interest in America and we will collect them from the Bank tomorrow'."

Donald put his hand up to his eyes.

There was more silence and then Salvia broke it by saying,

"Well, surely he could not do much harm just by reading the books."

"He said to me, 'if you are going to be away long you had better let me go to the Bank and collect the shares which I just know will make you a millionaire. As I am leaving very early you had better sign a cheque now for the amount of money you wish me to invest for you'."

No one spoke and Donald went on,

"I told him that he could only do so after he had looked at the books, but I did think that it would be rather a rush in the morning."

"So what did you do?" Salvia asked.

For a moment it was impossible for him to answer and then he said in a hoarse voice that did not sound like his own,

"I signed a cheque for him."

There was a horrified silence and then the Countess said,

"I don't understand at all. You signed a cheque, but was there anything wrong in that?"

"Apparently he added up everything that our money was invested in," Donald explained, "and took all that was in the Bank. And he took the shares of every Company that Papa had invested our money in."

"He drew it *all* out?" Salvia asked in amazement.

"All of it, everything that we possessed. I signed a cheque and the Bank never queried for a moment that it might be illegal."

"Are you saying," the Countess then asked after a moment's pause, "that we are left with nothing?"

"Practically nothing and the Bank says that he had forged a letter signing it with my signature, saying that he was to take from the Bank everything he asked for and his action had my complete approval."

"How could he do such a thing?" Salvia questioned, while the Countess was silent from sheer shock.

"I am sorry, so desperately sorry," Donald said. "I am leaving for America immediately to catch up with him and force him to give me back at least some if not all of our money."

"So do you mean he has stolen it for himself?" the Countess asked and her voice sounded almost strangled.

"I am afraid so, Mama, and I don't know how I can tell you how sorry I am. But I swear I will get at least some of it back. In fact I have told the servants to pack my clothes and I am leaving now for Southampton to catch the first ship going to America."

"Suppose he refuses to give you any of it back." Salvia asked.

"Then I will go to the Police and I feel that he has no wish to attract the unfavourable publicity that such a case would mean."

"I only hope you are right," Salvia said. "It seems to me just incredible that any man could behave in such an appalling manner even if he is a thief and a cad."

"I trusted him," Donald replied dismally, "because he was so friendly and amusing. I liked being with him but thought what I felt about him he felt about me."

"Instead he was stealing our all money," Salvia said speaking softly as if to herself.

"Do you really think, darling," the Countess said, "that you yourself can deal with this terrible man? Would it perhaps be wiser to have the advice from a good Solicitor here in England?"

"I think it would be a waste of time. If he is not to spend all of our money, then I must reach him as quickly as possible. Please forgive me, Mama, as I will never forgive myself."

He rose from the table and kissed his mother and then he hurried out of the room closing the door behind him.

Salvia looked at the Countess.

"How could this have happened?"

"I am asking the very same question," the Countess replied. "Does he really mean we now have no money?"

"I suppose the man managed to convince the Bank that that was our wish and they handed over everything we possessed," Salvia answered.

Then the Countess said,

"I suppose we will have to sell my jewellery. As the pictures and the furniture from both houses are entailed, I don't expect that Donald will be allowed to sell them even if he comes back penniless."

Salvia did not reply and after a moment her mother went on almost as if she was speaking to herself,

"Of course, I could close this house and I suppose, if nothing else, we could sell the horses which belong to Donald now that your father is dead."

"We are not going to sell anything at all until we are quite certain that Donald will not get our money back!" Salvia exclaimed.

"But if the money has all gone and we have nothing in the Bank," her mother replied, "how then are we going to live? After all the servants have to be paid. The food we eat does not come to us for nothing."

There was a long poignant silence and then Salvia said,

"We must now try hard to believe that this is only a temporary disaster and that Donald is right in thinking, if he reaches American soon after his friend, he will be able to retrieve at least some of the money back from him."

"I think you are being over-optimistic," her mother replied. "A thief is always a thief and he knew when he was taking the money away that we would be left penniless without it. But what do you think we should do now?"

"That is exactly what I am thinking about," Salvia murmured. "I am sure there is an answer to every problem if I can only find it."

"One thing which is quite obvious is that no one must be told about this debacle. We must keep it a secret until Donald returns. At the same time I am wondering if there is no money in the Bank, as he says, how can we pay the servants their wages or the shops for our food?"

"I have been thinking the same," Salvia admitted. "Of course we have a few things we can part with without anyone being aware that we are selling them."

"What do you mean by that?" her mother enquired at once.

"I mean we can pawn some of your jewellery and anything I own because they are ours. But we don't want to lose them. Pawning is better than selling and we have only a little time to find the money that will be needed by our household immediately."

The Countess put her hand up to her eyes.

"I cannot believe this is happening. It frightens me so much and I cannot imagine that there is any way out."

"You are not to despair, Mama, because the whole thing is so incredible and unbelievable. I keep thinking that there must be some way that we can save ourselves despite what Donald has done."

As she said his name the door opened and he came in.

"I am going to the Station, Mama," he said, "and I hope by tonight I will be well on my way to America."

"Oh, darling, are you right to go?" the Countess asked anxiously, standing up from the table.

She walked towards her son and put her hands on his shoulders.

"Are you wise to do this without asking advice?" she questioned. "We want to help in every way that we can and we will say nothing about it to anyone until you tell us that you can do no more."

"I knew I could rely on you, Mama," Donald said. "But our only chance is for me to catch up with him and make it clear that he must give me back the money. If not, then somehow I will force him to do so."

His mother did not speak and he added,

"You know how slow we are in England in dealing with things in other countries. The only way that I can circumvent Walter is by meeting with him before he either spends or transfers all our money into his own Bank."

"I am sure you are right about that," Salvia said. "I will look after Mama while you are gone, I promise."

"It deeply worries me that I have hurt her more than anything else," Donald replied.

He kissed his mother and then he said,

"Pray for me, Mama, and I will be as quick over this as I possibly can."

He smiled at his sister and ran down the passage and out of the front door where the carriage the servants had ordered for him was waiting to take him to the Railway Station.

Salvia put her arms around her mother.

"We have to trust him, Mama, and you must not make yourself unhappy. What is more important is that no one must be told about this. It must be a secret between ourselves and we cannot have all London laughing at us or worse still commiserating with us."

"You are quite right, darling," the Countess agreed.

There were tears in her eyes as she walked away to her sitting room and Salvia did not follow her.

Instead she went to the office, which was occupied by a secretary, who came in twice a week to pay the bills and to give the servants their wages.

It was a small room half-filled with tin boxes and there was a large writing table where the secretary usually sat.

Salvia knew where he kept the key to the safe.

She took it from a drawer and then opened the safe and, as she expected, there was a certain amount of money there, but not enough to pay the servants next Friday.

She knew that the secretary would want to draw out the money from the Bank and on the table waiting for him were a number of bills.

They were not large ones, but nevertheless enough to add up to quite a considerable amount of money.

As Salvia now knew there would be no money in the Bank to meet them.

'What can I do? What can I do?' she asked herself plaintively.

Then, as if it was a prayer sent up to Heaven to her father, she had the answer.

It seemed so strange that for a moment she thought that she must be imagining what she had just thought of.

Then she knew that there was one obvious answer to their present predicament.

If nothing else it would, if it worked, tide them over in the time that would elapse before Donald found Walter and returned home.

'It is possible, it really is possible,' she told herself.

Equally she could not help thinking that it was all somehow incredible.

Half an hour later Salvia, having changed from her riding clothes into one of the pretty and expensive dresses that her mother had bought for her, went downstairs.

Her hat trimmed with flowers made her look, she felt, very spring-like.

Their smart carriage would surely have returned by now after taking Donald to the Station and, without telling her mother where she might be going, she tip-toed past her bedroom and hurried down the stairs.

"When her Ladyship comes down and I know she is going out to luncheon," Salvia said to the butler, "tell her I was delayed this morning so I am late for an engagement and that is why I have not been able to come and to say 'goodbye' to her."

"I'll tell her Ladyship," the butler replied. "I hope your Ladyship enjoys yourself."

He looked admiringly at her pretty hat and dress.

She climbed into the carriage and gave the address.

She hoped that the butler, who had been with them for years and was rather deaf, would not hear her.

At the same time she told herself, as the carriage moved off, that he was not likely to connect it in any way with what she was actually doing.

It did not take the carriage long to reach the shop on Piccadilly where she had been on occasions with her father when they were travelling abroad.

Thomas Cook was a Company started twenty years ago for people who wished to travel abroad in comfort and wanted the best rooms in the very best hotels booked prior to their arrival.

It had been a new idea at the time which everyone had thought unnecessary, but now it was used by many people who found it very pleasant to be warmly welcomed as soon as they arrived at a foreign hotel.

Salvia gave her name as Lady Salvia Wenlock to the man at the door, saying that she wished to meet the Manager and was shown immediately into his office.

He was elderly with sharp intelligent eyes who rose to his feet as soon as she entered and held out his hand.

"It is delightful to see you, my Lady," he said. "I miss your father more than I can say."

"I miss him too," Salvia answered. "But now I need your help."

The Manager spread out his hands.

"Anything I can do for your Ladyship is, as you know, a pleasure," he told her.

Salvia sat down in front of his desk and began,

"I believe that you now arrange for people coming to England, especially from America, that they stay with a family instead of in a hotel. So they would be living in a house as if they were at their own home."

For a moment he looked rather puzzled and then he said,

"Actually we have had quite a number of enquiries of that sort from foreigners, who have a large family and prefer to take a whole house rather than stay in yet another hotel."

"That is what I thought you were doing," Salvia replied. "Now what I want you to find for me is someone distinguished in their own country and naturally very rich, who will pay a considerable sum to stay, not in a hotel, but at my brother's house, which as you well know is one of the finest houses in London."

She paused for a moment before she went on,

"With my dear mother always there to all intents and purposes the world will naturally think that the tenant is actually a friend of hers."

The Manager stared at her in some surprise and then he quizzed her,

"I am sorry if I seem to misunderstand, but are you suggesting that your mother, the Countess, would entertain these people as if they were friends and perhaps invite her own friends to meet them?"

Salvia nodded.

"Yes, that is just what I want, but it would be a very expensive arrangement and I will tell you, although it must go no further, that we need the money badly."

"I always believed that your father was a very rich man!" the Manager exclaimed.

"He was indeed, but at the moment my brother is in difficulties. In fact he has left for America to try to solve one or two problems. While he is away my mother and I have, unfortunately, practically nothing to live on."

She saw that he could not think of a suitable reply and she went on,

"I am telling you this in complete confidence and trust that it will go no further."

"That I can promise you, my Lady," the Manager answered. "But I can see that it is an extremely attractive proposition."

He smiled at Salvia.

"As a great number of people from other countries, especially Americans, are visiting England at present, I feel I should have no difficulty in finding a couple or perhaps two couples who would pay anything to be introduced to the Social world which they read about in the newspapers, but never thought it possible to be accepted into it."

He hesitated for a moment and then remarked,

"I am close friends with the American Embassy and they are often asking me for something new and interesting to introduce to their visitors. Frankly it is very difficult these days to think of anything new or different from what the average visitor always does when he or she pays a visit London."

"That is why," Salvia told him, "I thought we could let Wenlock House as one of the most famous in England, but, as my mother does not wish to move out, she could be their hostess. It would be a great attraction, especially to Americans who complain that we in England have all the heritage!"

The Manager laughed.

"That is true enough. I have heard them saying it a dozen times. Then they ask me for the impossible."

He smiled before he continued,

"At the moment my Lady, I think that is what you are offering me."

"Well, please arrange it as soon as possible," Salvia replied. "Of course, we should expect some money to be advanced so that we can provide the right food and see that the best rooms are made available to our guests."

The Manager rubbed his hands together.

"This is the most exciting and interesting project I have been offered for a very long time. In fact, my Lady, I think you are unique. It is surely a challenge that would have amused and gratified your father."

"I think that my father would have been interested because it is so unusual. That is what I think will attract your clients and I do not need to say that the sooner the whole business is in operation the better."

"I will start right away wiring America and finding out from their Embassy who is likely to be arriving in the next week or two," the Manager said excitedly. "If it is a success, I can only thank you, my Lady, from the bottom of my heart for bringing me something new and unusual."

Salvia rose to her feet.

"I knew that I could rely on you. I am so glad that Thomas Cook is here today. I really cannot imagine how difficult it must have been when you were not there to arrange everything for visitors from other countries."

"We do our best," the Manager said proudly.

He then escorted Salvia to her carriage and bowed respectfully as she drove away.

'That is one step in the right direction,' she said to herself. 'But now I have another one.'

She told the driver to take her home.

They arrived back quickly and then she dismissed the carriage.

When she entered the house, she ran upstairs to her bedroom.

She changed into the plain black clothes that she had worn when she was in mourning for her father and she put on the black hat which was very different from those covered with flowers and feathers sitting in the cupboard.

Then she put on the dark glasses that she had worn when she travelled abroad with her father to hot countries where he had always insisted that she protected her eyes from very bright sunlight.

Then she laughed at her reflection in the mirror and thought that she looked very business-like.

In fact nothing like the glamorous and lovely Lady Salvia, who the most dashing handsome gentlemen in London fought to dance with.

When no one was looking and the staff were either busy in the kitchen or upstairs in the bedrooms, she slipped out of the back door.

She walked towards Curzon Street as she knew that there was an Agency there which the butler used when he wanted another footman and the cook when she wanted more help in the kitchen.

She had always been told that it was the very best Agency in London.

There were several people sitting on seats at the end of the room waiting for jobs.

At the far end an elderly woman with grey hair was sitting at a high desk writing in a large book in front of her.

Salvia walked up to the desk and said,

"I have been told to come to you from the Countess of Wenlock. I helped her with a very difficult problem and now I require another job which she feels sure that you will be able to find for me."

"I am Mrs. Bailey and her Ladyship's quite right," she replied. "We've provided her with a great number of excellent servants over many years and she's always been grateful for our help."

"Very grateful indeed she has told me," Salvia said. "That is why I am sure, Mrs. Bailey, that you can help me to find what I require."

"What is it?"

"I am most fluent in languages and her Ladyship thought that I was wasted doing ordinary secretarial work when I should be assisting someone who is writing a book or who has a large amount of correspondence with foreign places."

Salvia paused before she added,

"Her Ladyship is certain that there are not many people on your books who can fulfil such a position."

"That's true enough, of course her Ladyship's right in thinking that people who are good at several languages are few and far between."

Salvia smiled.

"So please can you find me a job quickly, Mrs. Bailey otherwise there will be no reason for me to stay in London."

As if her urgency had an effect on her, Mrs. Bailey quickly turned over some of the pages of her book.

Another woman who had been listening to what was being said, who was sitting at a much lower desk, then rose to her feet and said in an audible whisper,

"What about Lord Carville?"

Mrs. Bailey drew in her breath.

"I'd forgotten about him, but, of course, this is what he's been asking for."

She turned towards Salvia.

"We have what's been to us a very difficult position where a gentleman is writing his book in three languages. He's asked us several times for an assistant but we've been unable to help with anyone who speaks three languages."

"I can understand that," Salvia remarked.

"But, of course, it's very unusual to find someone who can speak good French, Italian and Greek and I have a suspicion that his Lordship will be wanting other languages as well."

Salvia smiled.

"Well, I can do the first three at any rate," she said, "and I promise you that I am very fluent in all of them."

"Can you really say that when you are English?" Mrs. Bailey asked. "At least you look English."

"I am English," she told her. "But I have travelled in all those countries and, when I was with my father, he always insisted that I speak the local languages fluently."

Salvia paused and then went on,

"Otherwise, he said, one makes a million mistakes and misses a million things that are interesting and unusual in the countries you are visiting."

"Well, this is a surprise I'd not expected to have," Mrs. Bailey chuckled. "Will you please thank her Ladyship for sending you here?"

"I will most certainly," Salvia answered, smiling to herself. "But where should I go to meet this writer who is certainly very unusual?"

Mrs. Bailey then wrote out on a card what Salvia supposed was his name and address and, before she handed it to her, she asked.

"And what shall I say is your name?

Salvia has not been prepared for this and thought wildly.

Then she replied with the first name that came into her head,

"Miss Salvia More," she answered after her great-uncle Sandy More.

Mrs. Bailey wrote this down as well and passed the card over.

Salvia glanced at it before she asked,

"I should, of course, have enquired first what wages he will pay anyone who can meet his demands."

"That's what I've often said to my friend, but his Lordship decides the wages himself and discusses it only when he's employed the man or woman who he thinks is capable of doing his work."

"Oh, I see," Salvia replied.

She thought secretly that his Lordship had no wish to pay three people for doing the job of one.

Therefore she would certainly have to bargain with him and it was obviously something that Mrs. Bailey might find too difficult.

"I will go and see him at once," she said. "If he engages me, I will naturally let you know."

"If he does engage you," Mrs. Bailey replied, "then make certain that his Lordship and not you, pays for our fee."

"I will certainly remind him that that is his duty."

"I can only wish you well," Mrs. Bailey said, "and make it very clear that, if he doesn't find you exactly to his liking, we're not, at present, able to send him anyone else."

"I will make sure that his Lordship is aware that I am unique!" Salvia smiled. "Thank you very much and I will tell her Ladyship how kind you have been."

She walked to the door.

And when she was outside she read the address.

The carriage was waiting for her and she drove to Eton Square.

It was not a long journey.

In fact it was so near that Salvia thought that it was perhaps a mistake for them to see, as she was an applicant for a job, that she was arriving in a very smart carriage.

She therefore stopped the coachman at the entrance to the Square and told him that she would find her own way home.

"I have no idea how long I will be," she said, "and Her Ladyship might want you. I am almost sure that she is going out at teatime."

The coachman touched his hat and then the carriage drove off.

When it was out of sight, she walked to the side of the Square and found that the house where Lord Carville lived was at the far end.

The house was rather larger than the other houses and particularly beautiful.

Salvia thought that it had been built in 1600 and it was a perfect example of that period.

She rang the bell and the door was opened by a footman.

Salvia explained she had been sent by Mrs. Baily's Agency in answer to his Lordship's position for a linguist.

She was asked to wait in the hall while the butler, who appeared when she was showing the card that Mrs. Bailey had given her, took it from her and asked her to wait.

The footman pulled up a chair and she sat down demurely on it while she put on her glasses again.

When the butler returned, he said,

"If you'll come with me, miss, I'll take you to his Lordship."

They walked in silence down a long passage.

Then in a stentorian voice the butler announced,

"A young lady, my Lord, from the Agency."

Salvia walked in to what she saw at once was a comfortable study.

There were two full book cases and an impressive writing table with a gold ink-pot on it.

As it was full summer, the fireplace was filled with flowers and there was also a large arrangement of roses on a table which contained some fine pieces of china.

As she entered the room, a tall handsome man rose from the desk and greeted her,

"Good afternoon, Miss More, am I to gather that Mrs. Bailey has sent you here in answer to my request for someone who speaks three languages."

"That is correct, my Lord," Salvia replied. "As I speak all three of the languages fluently, I hope that you will find me suitable for the position."

For a moment she thought that his Lordship looked at her critically as if she was being impertinent.

Then without any warning he burst into French and spoke very fast in an obvious effort to intimidate her.

However, she managed, without difficulty, to speak as quickly, if not quicker, than he was.

Then he turned to Italian.

Although she had found the language difficult, she could speak it fluently because her father had often taken her there and insisted that she should speak it as well as he could.

Finally his Lordship began to speak in Greek.

This was a language that Salvia had always thought very attractive and always enjoyed speaking it.

Her voice was very soft as she answered him.

She finished with a description of Apollo and spoke of the reverence that the Greeks still gave him as the God of Love.

When she had finished, Lord Carville stared at her as if he could hardly believe that she was real.

"How is it possible," he asked, "when I have tried for so long to find someone to help me, that you suddenly appear and can speak the three languages that I have asked for, even better than I do myself?"

"I am not brave enough to say that," Salvia replied. "But I have always enjoyed being in those three countries and Greek particularly is, I really think, the most attractive language in the whole of Europe."

"You are quite right," Lord Carville agreed. "I have always felt that myself, but I found it impossible to engage anyone to help me with the books I am writing."

"But why, if you will forgive me asking," Salvia began, "are you writing three books at the same time in three languages?"

"It's the same book," Lord Carville explained, "but if I translate it as I go along, it saves a great deal of delay afterwards. That is what I find boring, but I cannot entirely trust a secretary to express what I wish to express and any alteration in my mind would spoil what I am trying to put into words."

Salvia smiled.

"I suppose all authors think that anyone else will spoil the words that they know are correct and essential for what they are trying to convey."

"You are quite right," Lord Carville agreed. "Now I require you to come to me here from ten o'clock in the morning until four o'clock in the afternoon."

Salvia nodded.

"I can do that, my Lord, but, of course, I must ask you what you will be paying me for my services."

She felt slightly embarrassed at saying this.

But Lord Carville made a gesture with his hands.

"What do you want?" he asked. "I obviously want you, so I am not going to argue over pounds, shillings and pence."

"That is exactly what I hoped you would say."

Salvia quoted what she felt was quite a large figure for what she would be doing. And it would surely help to pay the staff not only in London but also in the country.

His Lordship then replied,

"I expected that you would be expensive which you undoubtedly are. But, as you are unique and I cannot find anyone else, I expect you to be here tomorrow morning at ten promptly."

"I only hope that I am able to help your Lordship and I am a very punctual person."

Salvia rose to her feet and Lord Carville rose to his.

He stood looking at her and then said,

"Surely you are very young to have learnt so much, Miss More. Perhaps you will find correcting what I have written to be more difficult than you anticipated."

"Are you saying in a polite way," Salvia asked him, "that you do not want me?"

"Of course not," he answered hastily. "I want you desperately simply because I do have not the time to waste going over my own work once I have done it and I cannot trust those they have sent me, who have no idea of giving the world what I want in three volumes."

"I think it is rather amusing, my Lord, I will enjoy it if I do find something wrong simply because you are different from any other author who puts his feelings into words in one language let alone three."

"I don't have time to waste on doing it slowly and to be honest I want to be back on my travels. Therefore the sooner I can finish these three books I have promised to each of the countries I have visited, the quicker I can be off again looking for more and perhaps better excitement that I have found already."

Salvia laughed.

"You are certainly very ambitious and so I can only promise that I will help you to the best of my ability."

"That is all I am asking for. I am finding it hard to believe that you know so much and will understand exactly what I am trying to convey to the people these books are written for."

"In which case I can only try, but I feel sure that we will do it elegantly and without any disagreeableness."

She said this in Greek and the words seemed to be almost a poem in themselves.

"If you dare to leave me now," Lord Carville said, "I will search London for you as I realise that you are exactly what I want and what I was afraid I would never be able to find."

"I will be here at ten o'clock tomorrow morning," Salvia promised, "and thank you for accepting me."

She walked towards the door as she was speaking, opened it and, before he could find words to answer her with, she was gone.

He put his hand up to his forehead.

"I think I am dreaming!" he exclaimed aloud to the fire.

## CHAPTER TWO

When she reached home, Salvia realised that she had to tell her mother all that she had arranged today and she knew that it would be rather difficult.

But she informed the Countess that she had been to Thomas Cook's and that they would be sending her some Americans who would want to be, if possible, presented to some of the influential people in London.

The Countess then stared at her quizzically as she finished speaking.

"Am I hearing you right?" she asked. "Surely you cannot expect me to have people in the house who I know nothing about, who are foreigners and then expect me to introduce them to my friends."

She spoke in a voice that she used when she was not only astonished but insulted by what she had heard.

"I am sorry, Mama, but if we have no money, the alternative is to shut up this house, sack all the servants and very likely have to do the same in the country."

The Countess put her hand up to her eyes.

"This just cannot be true, I am quite certain that I am dreaming. Surely your brother has not taken all our money after all."

"He has not, but his friend has," Salvia replied. "I promise, Mama, that we have to be very brave and face this in a way that will give us as little misery as possible."

She hesitated a little before she added,

"You know as well as I do that you would hate to sack all the servants, who have been with us for so long and who have been so faithful."

There was silence as neither of them spoke.

At last the Countess, in a voice which did not sound at all cheerful, sighed,

"I suppose I will have to do what you want me to."

"It is not what I want, but what we *have* to do. I think it might be quite amusing. It will be something new at any rate and you yourself have often said that we do the same old things over and over again and entertain the same people who entertain us."

Another pause and then the Countess said,

"I suppose I must accept the inevitable, but I think your father would be shocked at the idea at me having to entertain people I have never even met."

"I think Papa would be the one person who would take this with a laugh and, as you heard him say so often, 'it is something new and we might as well try it'."

The Countess managed to smile.

"Yes, he said it often, but not over things like this," she murmured.

"But it is what he felt and what we must feel at this moment," Salvia answered with a faint smile. "We have to do the impossible because otherwise the alternative will be inevitable."

She stood up and walked to the window to gaze out at the garden.

It struck her, as it had done before, that it would break their hearts if they had to give up this lovely house, which had been in the family for so long and was the envy of all their friends.

"Your house is unique," she had heard a visitor say. "I never imagined that there would be such a lovely house in the centre of London. No wonder you are so proud of it."

'Not only proud,' Salvia thought now, 'but we are so terrified of losing it. Please, please God let us stay here and not have to go anywhere else.'

Even as she said her prayer, she was thinking of the horses in the country and the dogs who had always meant so much to her.

'If Donald does not get back any of our money,' she thought, 'they will all have to go.'

The whole idea was so frightening that she tried not to think about it. Yet it was hovering just like a dark cloud over everything she said and everything that she might be thinking.

They had luncheon and inevitably the chef tried to tempt them with some delicious new dishes that they had not tasted before.

Salvia felt that he at any rate would rather enjoy having more people in the house and more parties to cope with than they had at the moment.

'If these people from abroad want us to entertain them,' she thought, 'I see no reason why we should not do so. There is no point in telling our friends we are broke and that is the reason why we have to have strangers in the house.'

Of course she was vitally concerned with all the inevitable problems.

'We will just pretend they are friends of friends,' she thought, 'and that is why we do not know them well. In fact we are doing them a kindness having them to stay in one of the finest houses in London and then meeting the most alluring, amusing and attractive members of the *Beau Monde*.'

But while she was being optimistic even to herself, she was really frightened.

Frightened it might all be a disaster and even more frightened that Donald would not be able take back any of the money that had been stolen from him.

Later she told her mother gently that she had some work to do the next day and so would not be able to join her for luncheon.

"I will return as soon as I can," Salvia promised. "But remember, Mama, that his Lordship is paying for my services and I am quite certain that I will earn every penny by sheer hard work!"

The Countess patted her daughter's cheek.

"You are very brave, darling, and I am so proud of you," she smiled and Salvia kissed her.

When they went up the stairs, her lady's maid was waiting to undress the Countess.

She had been with them for over twenty years and Salvia thought that it would be a complete disaster if she had to leave.

'Mama would miss her more than I could put into words,' she thought. 'She has always taken such care of her and her clothes.'

Then she told herself that she must stop thinking of how disastrous it could be.

She believed that her new ideas would work and the one person who must not suffer from losing all their money would be her dear mother.

'I must be so sure in my own mind that everything will come right,' she thought to herself, 'and I must stop being so afraid.'

As she climbed into bed, she was worried simply as it was too great a disaster for anyone as inexperienced as herself to be able to prevent from happening.

She then said a special prayer for her brother and she was sure that by now he would be well on his way to America.

Then a prayer to her father who she knew would have made the same arrangements as she had done, if he had been alive to do so.

'I am sure that Thomas Cook's will give us some nice people, Papa. I know, thanks to the education you made me have, I will be able to please Lord Carville and that at least will earn us some much needed money.'

Then she remembered that she had not really found out what salary Lord Carville would agree to pay her and she only hoped that it would be large enough to pay the wages for at least three of the servants or perhaps four.

Then she told herself she must try to go to sleep.

Otherwise her brain would not be working as well as expected and his Lordship would be disappointed in her and perhaps give her the sack.

She therefore closed her eyes and went on praying quietly until she fell into a deep asleep.

*

She woke with a jerk and saw the daylight coming in through the sides of the curtain and knew that it was now morning.

When she looked at the clock, she was surprised to find that it was just eight o'clock and she had indeed slept peacefully.

When the maid came in, she said,

"I am going out at half-past nine, so will you tell them that I will have my breakfast in round about twenty minutes."

Salvia dressed herself in the plain sensible clothes that she had worn yesterday, which she thought made her look like a secretary.

She had difficulty with her hair because she knew that she would have to take off her hat when she arrived at his Lordship's house.

Her fair curls, that had always been much admired, would not keep themselves in the straight neat and tidy way which she felt would be expected from one if his hired workers.

However, she hurried because she wanted to look in the library where she was sure that there were books which had been put there by her father in case she stumbled over the three languages that Lord Carville was writing his book in.

'I wonder what it is about,' she thought. 'Perhaps he is describing his visits to foreign lands. Or is it possible that he has written a book which concerns love?'

Somehow she felt this unlikely and she only hoped that whatever subject his Lordship had chosen she would not be completely ignorant about it.

She glanced at her father's French books and then at the Italian ones which were either travel guides or the classics that she had never read.

Then she came at the far end of one of the shelves to the books about Greece.

These were old friends.

She felt as soon as she opened one of the books that the words seemed to fly out at her and give her a sense of happiness and love that she had always connected with the history of the Gods and Goddesses and the description of Ancient Greece itself.

She had travelled there once with her father and she thought that she would never forget how moving she had felt the whole country to be.

She had been certain that the Gods and Goddesses were still there even though one was unable to see them.

'I will love helping his Lordship with this book,' she thought, 'even if I find that the other two are more difficult.'

She picked out certain passages from the book on Greece and then glanced at the clock on the mantelpiece.

It was nearly half-past nine and, if she was to be punctual, as it was easier to walk than to take a carriage, she ought to leave immediately.

She ran up the stairs to her mother's bedroom, as the Countess usually had breakfast in bed.

"Good morning, darling," she greeted her.

"Good morning, Mama. I have to hurry as I have to be at the place where I am working at ten o'clock."

"I thought in the night you had not yet told me who you were working for or what you were doing."

"I will tell you tonight, but I am looking to you to make my excuses to your friends at luncheon today."

Then the Countess said,

"You know how I hate telling lies, but I suppose it would be a great mistake to say you are working because we had lost our money."

"Of course, it would, Mama, and don't breathe a word especially in front of the servants. We must play our parts as if we are experienced actresses."

Her mother laughed.

"Very well, darling, I will act my part and make your excuses for not coming to the luncheon party, although I am sure that the young men who are usually there will be very disappointed that I have come alone."

"Give them my love and say I hope to see them as soon as possible," she answered. "There is no reason why we should not accept invitations in the evening. In fact it will save money being spent at home, but then no one must have the slightest suspicion that everything is not as happy and complete with us as it has always been."

The Countess gave a deep sigh.

"I will do my very best, darling, but it is going to be difficult to keep people from knowing that things are not right with us."

"I can see no reason," Salvia said firmly, "why they should guess that we are completely bankrupt. And do not tell them that Donald has gone to America as they might think that is strange when there is so much for him to do at home."

She smiled and added,

"We must be very brave as if things are perfectly ordinary except that we will have visitors in the house and, because they are foreigners, there will be every excuse not to make them too familiar with our friends."

"You have an answer to everything," the Countess replied. "But I can only pray that things will go smoothly and no one will catch us out."

"I am sure that we are going to win and that is what you must keep saying to yourself. This is a battle we will win and in a very short time our life will go on exactly the same as it has in the past."

As she finished speaking, Salvia bent forward and kissed her mother.

"I love you, Mama. You know that Papa would dismiss all these difficulties with a wave of his hand and that is exactly what we have to do."

"You are right, darling, of course you are right. At the same time I cannot help feeling apprehensive. It would break my heart to have to leave this house or our home in the country."

"I know. That is why we have to fight to keep it all and that is what we are going to do. We are going to win!"

She kissed her mother once again and before the Countess could say anything more, Salvia had gone out of the room closing the door behind her.

Fortunately she had put her things ready before she went downstairs for breakfast.

Picking up the rather plain hat she had worn the day before, she put it on her head in the hall and then she put the glasses that she had worn yesterday into her handbag.

There was only one footman in the hall to let her out and, as he was young and fairly new, he did not seem at all surprised that she would be walking to her destination and did not require a carriage.

When she thought that the horses in the stables and the three grooms who looked after them might have to go, she felt just as if a dagger was being plunged deep into her heart.

How could they possibly part with everything that was so familiar and which meant so much to them?

She told herself that she was being weak instead of strong and she had to believe that this was just a bad dream which would pass away very shortly.

Nevertheless she could not help thinking about the large amount of money that was needed to keep the house going and to pay all the servants. Besides the even larger expenses of the house and estate in the country.

How was it possible, just how was it credible that everything could vanish so quickly?

Yes, she had to face the fact that at the moment they had nothing in the Bank.

It did not take her long to reach Lord Carville's house in Eton Square.

A footman opened the door and smiled when he saw who was standing outside.

"Good mornin', Miss More," he began. "You're ever so punctual which is a lot more than the last secretary was."

Salvia smiled.

"I hate being late, just as I am sure his Lordship dislikes having to wait."

"You can be sure of that," he replied. "When we runs to answer his bell, he always says we've been a long time in comin', even if we ain't."

He smiled at Salvia.

"His Lordship'll be in the library and I'll tell him you're in his study and if anyone's late it be him!"

"I don't believe you are brave enough to say that," Salvia said, "even if it is true."

The footman giggled and opened the study door.

She then took off her hat thinking that perhaps she should have done so before and put it quickly behind the sofa.

'I must remember to behave as if I was a servant, rather than a lady calling on a gentleman,' she thought to herself.

There was a mirror over the fireplace and she tidied her hair until in a few minutes she heard footsteps coming along the corridor.

The door opened and Lord Carville walked in and, seeing her by the mantelpiece, he smiled and said,

"Well, you are punctual and that is the first step we need in getting these books finished and out of our way."

"I have been thinking about that," Salvia said. "I am hoping that they will be a huge success and I am sure they will be."

"Why are you so sure?" Lord Carville asked.

"I am sure that you want to give people who read them something which will help and inspire them," Salvia answered, "and that is what everyone wants from a book if they cannot obtain it from the people around them."

Lord Carville stared at her.

"I have never thought of that before. Do you really believe that I am writing books that will actually help the people who read them?"

"It is what they should do. Every book we read has an effect on our minds and those which really matter help us to live a little better than we have lived before."

Again Lord Carville stared at her.

"You must tell me more. I suppose, from the way you are speaking, you must have read a great number of books."

"I love reading and I have been reading ever since I was five or six years old. Your library is, I am sure, a very fine one, but so is ours."

She spoke without thinking and then realised that it would not be usual for a young woman, who had to earn her living, to have a large library.

Because she saw surprise in his Lordship's eyes, she said quickly,

"Now I think, my Lord, that we should get down to working. What will make it easier for me to help you is if you read me a little from one of your books, which will give me some idea about what you are aiming to convey to your readers."

"I suppose that is a sensible suggestion," he said. "I had not thought of it before. But, of course, if you are to help me as I need to be helped, I want these books to be different from all the usual rubbish that is found in foreign libraries."

He coughed before he went on,

"I had not thought that the people I am writing for would be either inspired or educated by what I give them in my books."

"But it is what you really want even if you did not think of it," Salvia replied. "Every book that we read has a real effect on our mind, our character and perhaps as well our future."

She smiled at him before continuing,

"Therefore, if you have a serious book, as I imagine your Lordship's will be, it must be exciting as well so that people will reach up to the sky because they have read what you have written."

For a moment there was silence.

And then he said,

"Let's get down to brass tacks. I thought if you sat at my desk you would be able to take down in shorthand, if you can do it, what I dictate. Then you can translate it into the other languages as quickly as possible."

He stopped before he went on,

"To put it more simply, I suggest that I dictate in French and we can then unite in translating what I have said into Italian and Greek. With luck it will not take as long as most people take when they write a book. In fact I am told the usual time is a year before a book is completely finished."

"As that all depends on the writer, I think we would be very ashamed of ourselves if we took as long as that. If you could give me the first chapter now in French, we will see how long it takes and we can work out approximately how long we have to work before the book is finished."

"Very well, let's start," Lord Carville answered.

Salvia then slipped off her coat thinking that it was something she should have done in the hall.

'I must not make this mistake again,' she thought as she sat down at the desk.

There was a pile of paper ready for her on the table and a collection of pens and pencils.

She picked up a pencil because she thought that it was easier and quicker to write with, rather than to keep dipping the pen into an ink-pot.

She waited as his Lordship sat down near the table.

Now he started dictating slowly to her in French.

She had thought that perhaps he would speak of his journeys to France and she rather expected him to describe some of the beauties of that country.

To her astonishment Lord Carville started with the history of all the various countries in the world.

How each is affecting the others by fighting and by inventing their own patriotic ideals.

He spoke on Parliamentary Democracy, which had been first introduced in England and had been copied by France, but had never, up to now, been really effective in Greece.

Then he spoke of the development of man over the ages and the very first steps of civilisation.

It was all very highbrow and she thought that, while some people would think it interesting, many would feel that there was nothing in it for themselves.

She had done about four pages when to her surprise Lord Carville remarked,

"Now before we go any further I want you to tell me if you think that will be particularly interesting when it is translated into Italian and Greek."

There was silence for a moment and then she asked him,

"Do you want the truth or shall I be polite and say how clever I think you are?"

"I am delighted to hear that you think I am clever," Lord Carville replied. "Therefore why should I be afraid of the truth?"

"It is not for me to criticise what you are writing," Salvia said slowly. "But I am wondering what effect you think that this piece you have just written will have on the people who read it?"

"I have been asked for a book and I think they will find my thoughts very interesting when I travel and these I intend to put in, in more detail, further on."

He was looking at Salvia as he spoke.

"Tell the truth! You are not really impressed with what I have given you so far, are you?"

"If you want the truth," Salvia replied, "I am afraid that you might be angry with me for saying it."

Lord Carville did not speak and she continued,

"I would indeed like to tell you what I think, but I am afraid that you will dismiss me immediately."

"As I had a great difficulty in finding you, you may be quite certain that I have no wish to lose you now."

"Very well, then I must risk you being angry with me. I think that what you are giving the readers, who have asked for your book, is not really what they want."

Lord Carville looked surprised.

"Then what do they want?" he asked.

"I think they want something that will please them about their own country and to help them individually."

"How can I possibly do that when each country is so different?" Lord Carville asked.

"That, if you will forgive me for saying so, is just where you have gone wrong," Salvia answered. "Because you dictate so quickly, I know that a book from you would not take half so long as people who sit holding their heads and thinking out every word before they say it."

She hesitated for a moment before she added,

"What a reader requires from you is something very different."

She looked at Lord Carville to see if he was angry.

His eyes were now on her and she saw that he was listening to what she was saying.

"What I think all these people want from you," she went on, "is just what everyone wants. That is they want inspiration and encouragement in themselves."

"Why do you say that?"

"Because it is the truth. You are important, you are good-looking, you are English and you have a title. You are known by many people in the world and even those you have not met have doubtless heard about you."

There was silence before Salvia went on,

"What they will want from you is not what you are giving them which, if you will forgive me for saying so, is rather dull and far too intelligent for the average person to assimilate."

"What then do they want from me?" he asked.

It was quite obvious that he was rather annoyed by what Salvia was saying.

"I am risking my job by being frank," Salvia said. "But I have visited the countries you are writing about. I have talked to the people, although maybe not such grand persons as you have associated with."

She paused before she went on,

"I know what they would love is your impression of the country and its people and your inspiration for them to do better for themselves in the future. To do better and to give them the feeling of what each one could acquire if they tried."

Lord Carville drew in his breath and replied,

"How could I possibly do that in one book?"

"You cannot," Salvia replied. "You have to give the French the French book, the Italians the Italian and the Greeks a really wonderful book that the Gods could write better than you are able to do."

Only as she said the words that came instinctively to her lips, did she realise that she was being rude.

She put up her hands to say,

"Forgive me! I have been carried away by what I am thinking and I should not have said that."

"Of course, you should say it," he retorted. "I like frankness and, while you are entirely different from anyone else who has worked for me, I realise that you are telling me things that I ought to have thought of for myself."

There was then a poignant silence between the two of them before Salvia observed,

"The French are so different from other countries. The French want to be amused. They want to laugh. They want to be told that their women are attractive and the most alluring in the whole world."

She smiled as she carried on,

"And so their sense of humour percolates out from their country and everyone who pays a visit to France goes back feeling invigorated and entranced."

She paused and then continued,

"Not only by the beauty of it, but that the people are such great fun and so delightful that one is continually laughing. They raise the spirit of everyone who travels in France. It is difficult in that country to be unhappy."

She spoke quickly and then looked at Lord Carville again afraid that he would tell her that she was a fool and dismiss her for impertinence.

Then he asked her quietly,

"What do I say to Greece?"

"You say exactly what is in your heart and what you yourself know about love. Love to the Greeks is the same as sunshine is other people."

He was listening intently and she went on,

"They live in their own world and have inspired the world outside with their ideals and their knowledge of all that is ultimately the best and highest in a man's soul. And how eventually he can find the love that only the Gods can give us."

She spoke softly and there was a little tremor in her voice at the end and after a pause she concluded,

"The Gods and Goddesses of Greece have brought love to the world. Although people are shy to admit it, it is what they are seeking."

There was silence before Lord Carville responded,

"You are right! Of course, you are right! I should have thought of this myself. But now that you have told me what is wanted, I am quite certain that I could write, as you have described, a book for every country that will help and inspire them, as they have never been before."

"You understand, you really do understand!" Salvia exclaimed.

"Of course, I understand. It just never occurred to me that these three countries should want from me what I always imagined their teachers and Priests were giving to their people."

"One cannot have too much of a good thing," she said softly. "Because they admire you and think because you are English that you are different in many ways, what you say will not only surprise them but encourage them to reach out to something higher and better than themselves."

Then Lord Carville said,

"How could I have been such a fool as to think I could put all that into one book or that the three different countries would each understand it? You are quite right, of course, you are right, we must give them what they want to hear and what will inspire them!"

Salvia smiled.

"And you are not angry with me?"

"Of course, I am not angry! I am only glad that you came to my rescue before I made a fool of myself."

"I am certain, my Lord, that you could never be a fool. But you were asking too much of people who are incapable of understanding what you are saying."

"I realise that now. So let's go to rock bottom and I will write a book that you will be proud of and so I am prepared to let you choose which will be the first."

Salvia thought for a moment.

"The most difficult and the one that I feel will have the most impact is a book to Italy. They do not seem to understand the working of the spirit and the soul as we understand it because we have learnt it from the Greeks."

She thought again before she continued,

"So I think you should start with France, which is the easiest one. Then, if I am still with you, we can tackle Italy and lastly, as it will be a joy and delight which is hard to express in words, we will do Greece."

"You are right, I am sure that you are right!" Lord Carville exclaimed. "So let's get going and I feel as if you are putting the very words into my mouth."

"They might well be in your mouth, my Lord, but they have to come from your heart and your soul. That is the only way you can give the people, who are waiting for these books, what they hope they will find."

Lord Carville sighed.

"I am quite certain that you are not a human being but an angel sent down from Heaven to help me."

# CHAPTER THREE

Three days later when Salvia arrived home after a long afternoon session with Lord Carville, she found her mother waiting for her.

"What do you think, darling?" she said. "Thomas Cooks have sent me a message to say that Mr. and Mrs. Melton and their two children, who I gather are grown up, will be arriving here tomorrow afternoon."

"Well, they have not taken very long about it, have they Mama!"

"I did not believe that they would come almost at once," her mother answered. "But they are paying such an enormous sum that I can hardly tell you about it because I think it must be a dream."

She held out the letter from Thomas Cooks as she spoke and, when Salvia saw it, she gave a whoop of joy.

"That is a lot. I never thought that we would get as much as that."

"They have really done us proud," her mother said, "in making the Americans pay so much, but, of course, this house is exceptional."

Salvia was staring at the piece of writing paper her mother had passed to her as if she was afraid that it might fade away and become part of her imagination.

"This will enable us to pay the servants for at least six months and those in the country as well. Oh, Mama, we are lucky, but, of course, you will have to bear the brunt of it as I shall be out working. But I am sure that you will find them very congenial if nothing else."

The Countess laughed.

"We can only hope so. At the same time it was so very clever of you, darling, to think of anything so helpful. I was in complete despair that we would have to sack our loyal servants."

"Forget it, Mama, our dream has come true and we will be able to keep our heads above water until Donald finds that ghastly friend of his."

"I am sure that my prayers have been answered," the Countess replied. "For the moment everything can go on as it has in the past."

"I wonder what these people are like," Salvia said. "I am sure that they must be very rich to pay so much for staying in our house. That means we should give them a warm welcome whatever they look like or however they behave."

"You are not now suggesting that they will behave badly?" the Countess asked. "After all they must realise that if they are staying with me they must be on their best behaviour."

"Of course, they will, darling Mama," Salvia said reassuringly.

Bending down she kissed her on the cheek.

"Everyone behaves well when you are there," she told her mother. "So, don't let's be afraid, but give them a warm welcome."

Almost as an afterthought she asked,

"Does this letter tell us the ages of their son and daughter?"

She looked at the letter as she spoke and found that Mr. Melton had put in that his son was aged twenty-two and his sister eighteen.

Well, at least they will enjoy any party we plan for them," Salvia commented aloud.

47

"That is what I was thinking," her mother replied. "But perhaps it would be wise if we had a look at them first in case people think it very odd that we should entertain such strange beings and then find out about Donald."

"They must never do that as they would then pity us and Donald would be furious if it was known that he had been taken in by a crook."

"Of course, he would be," her mother agreed at once. "That is why we must be very careful."

Salvia, however, thought it more practical to make out a list of the people who had asked her to a party and who she knew well enough to ask if she might bring some friends who were staying with them.

'I will not do anything until I have seen them,' she told herself. 'Equally, as they will be paying so much, they must have their money's worth and we must entertain them royally.'

As she went upstairs to change for dinner she was thinking about Lord Carville and his books more than the Americans.

They had worked for the last two days on his book for France and she thought that he had really made it very interesting in exactly the way that the French would expect and enjoy.

She found it amusing to try to cap his stories with some of her own.

She was surprised when he accepted so many of her suggestions instead of brushing them aside and so make it obvious that he knew better than she did.

'I like him,' she thought, 'and it is very strange for a man as young as he is to want to help people in other countries rather than just enjoy himself selfishly when he is abroad.'

But she did feel tired when the following afternoon Lord Carville went to a Race Meeting and she typed from the time she arrived until the time she left his house in the late afternoon.

'I feel that my head is buzzing and my fingers are stiff,' she mused. 'Now I must go home and make the last preparations for these Americans who will be arriving at our house tomorrow.'

She could not help a little shiver just in case things went wrong and that would upset her mother.

Then they would have to turn them out and give back the money that they had been promised.

Actually some of the money had arrived in advance as she had opened a letter from Thomas Cook's, which was addressed to her and she had been thrilled when she saw the cheque inside it.

'How could I have thought of anything so useful?' she asked herself. 'I am sure Papa, wherever he might be now, is helping me.'

Nevertheless, when she had changed into one of her pretty dresses and she and her mother were waiting in the drawing room for their visitors, she could not help feeling a little intimidated.

'Suppose they are ghastly?' she asked herself. 'As we have no men, as neither Papa nor Donald is with us, I will have to be the one to tell them that they must leave our house.'

Then she told herself that it was a great mistake to be pessimistic.

Just as she had managed to inspire Lord Carville, she should be able to inspire the Americans into doing and saying the right thing.

Nevertheless she felt a little breathless when, just before tea, she heard the sound of voices in the hall.

Just a few minutes later the drawing room door was opened and the butler in a stentorian voice announced to her and her mother,

"My Lady, Mr. and Mrs. Melton, Miss Mary-Lee and Mr. Shelby."

Just for a moment it seemed as if the people coming into the room swam before her eyes and it was difficult to look at them.

Then she heard the young American boy saying out loud,

"Gee, this mansion sure be the tops. I'll bet my last cent on that!"

Salvia heard her mother laugh and then she laughed too.

Now, as they moved forward she could see that Mr. Melton was a tall good-looking man with grey hair.

His wife was dressed in fashionable and expensive clothes and so was his daughter.

His son, who had just expressed himself in a very American way, was also good-looking, but obviously very American with his closely-cropped hair.

"Welcome to England," the Countess was saying charmingly. "I do hope that we will make you very happy here."

Next she was shaking hands with Mrs. Melton and Salvia followed.

"We thought your house would be big," Mr. Melton said, "and we were told just how significant it has been in British history, but it still surprises me. May I congratulate you, ma'am, on owning anything so fine?"

"I am delighted to hear you say that," the Countess replied. "Do please sit down and tell me if you had a good voyage and I hope that the sea was not too rough."

"I am afraid I felt rather seasick," Mrs. Melton said, "but my son and daughter enjoyed themselves and we were very comfortable on the English ship."

"We thought as we were coming to England," Mr. Melton explained with a smile, "we would travel English and learn a little about you all."

"I hope that what you learnt was in our favour," the Countess enquired.

"Very much so," Mr. Melton replied, "and I think next time that I leave America it will undoubtedly be on an English ship."

"My father found them to be more comfortable than those belonging to any other country," Salvia said.

"I was told that your father was very famous," the American remarked. "The Captain of the ship told me a lot about him and I'm real sorry that he could not be here to welcome us as you have done."

Salvia longed to say that if her father had been here there would not be any need for them to entertain strange people who were paying their way.

Instead she said,

"We hope you will find England as delightful and as entrancing as you think it will be. My mother is going to introduce you to many of her friends, who I think you will find charming. And, of course, there is so much for you to see in London and in the countryside."

"We are looking forward to it," Mr. Melton replied. "My wife and I are hoping that our daughter, Mary-Lee, will be asked to some of the balls we have read about in the newspapers and magazines, which are very different, I feel sure, from the dance parties we have in New York."

"Is that where you live?" Salvia asked. "I always think New York sounds such a fascinating City and I hope to visit it one day."

"You must come and stay with us," he replied.

While they were talking, as it was now too late for tea, the butler brought in drinks which he passed round.

Salvia thought that Mr. Melton and his son drank their drink far too quickly.

In fact they swilled it down and then asked to have their glasses filled again and it was not a very strong drink.

She thought they were rather greedy in drinking it so quickly and then reproached herself for being critical.

"I feel sure that you would like my mother to tell you about the party you are going to tomorrow," she said. "We thought that tonight you would be too tired after your journey and would have dinner here and then retire to bed early."

Mrs. Melton nodded.

"But tomorrow we have planned quite a lot for you to see," Salvia continued, "and, if it is very different from what you have in New York, I feel that will make it more interesting for you because it will be something new."

"We will enjoy anything you offer us," Mr. Melton said, before the rest of his family could speak.

Then his daughter, Mary-Lee, piped up,

"I want to dance. I am told that the men in England dance better than the men in America and I love dancing."

"I want to ride," her brother told them. "I hear your horses are exceptional and, although I have several horses of my own, I have often felt that they are not as fine as they ought to be."

"You will have to wait until we go to the country to try our best horses," Salvia replied. "But we have horses of our own in the stables here and you can ride in Rotten Row in Hyde Park if you want to try them out."

"I fancy myself on an English horse," he said, "and I bet I beat you, Miss Wenlock, if you will race me."

"That will take place in the country, which we will go to any week that suits you," Salvia replied. "But your sister particularly wants to dance at London parties where she will meet the English girls of the same age."

They were all listening as Salvia went on,

"My mother has arranged for her to be invited to several large balls which are being held next week."

"That is real kind of you," Mr. Melton said to the Countess. "It's just what I might expect of you and your husband, who was so much respected in America."

"I am very glad that they have not forgotten him," the Countess answered.

Mrs. Melton heard the throb in her voice and said,

"You must not think that we have not heard of his Lordship. But as it happens my father heard him speaking once and thought that he was a very clever man. So I can well understand how much you miss him."

The Countess was obviously very touched by this.

Salvia then suggested,

"If you have finished your drinks, perhaps before you go to dress for dinner you would like to see the Picture Gallery. We have a music room here as well and you must persuade my mother or me to play you some of the tunes which are most popular in London at the moment."

Mr. Melton voted for the Picture Gallery which was also used as a ballroom and the pictures were superb.

Salvia had not taken anyone round it without them exclaiming at the largeness of the collection and the beauty and antiquity of the pictures

Mr. Melton went round in silence and she realised that he had no idea that he was looking at pictures from the greatest artists who had ever painted or that he should be stunned by their beauty.

His daughter was clearly bored and hardly glanced at the pictures as she was looking at the room purely as a place to dance.

"How many dances will you be giving here while we are staying with you?" she asked.

"I think my mother has arranged three," Salvia told her, "and you will be attending balls in other houses and smaller dances which I have found are much more fun than the big ones."

"Do you think that I will have a partner if I go to them?" Mary-Lee asked Salvia.

"Of course, you will. It is my job to see that you dance every dance and I am certain if you wear a pretty dress and have your hair arranged fashionably, you will be the belle of the ball and every man will be fighting to be your partner."

"I cannot expect as much as that," she answered. "But I love dancing and really want to dance with English men who dance so well."

"Not as good as the French," Salvia said, thinking of what she had been writing that day with Lord Carville.

"In that case I'm sure I'd like France," Mary-Lee said. "I asked Papa if he would take us to Paris, but he and Mama were so keen to come to England because they think the English are the smartest people socially in the world."

"That is a lovely compliment and one I will always remember. But you must wait and when you have enjoyed the parties tell me if you think any other country would do them better than we do."

Mary-Lee laughed.

"Even if I thought it I would be too frightened to say so to you," she replied.

"I do like people who are frank," Salvia said. "And from what I have read and heard I think that Americans are very forthright about their likes and dislikes."

"That be true enough," Shelby Melton said who had been listening to their conversation. "I want to say I think you are swell and I'll bet my last cent by saying I am sure none of those Frenchies are as pretty as you."

Salvia was rather surprised at the compliment, but she merely laughed and thanked him for it.

When she went upstairs to change for dinner, she showed them the superb bedrooms that had been allotted to them.

"This one is called the 'King Charles II room'," she said, "because it is reported that he slept here just as in the country there is also a Charles II bedroom."

"That be real smart," Shelby said. "But I doubt if I'll ever be a King."

His sister laughed.

"Of course, you will not, Shelby, but ever since you were a little boy you have always wanted to be King of the Castle. Well, now you can show all the English that we Americans are not as stupid as they believe us to be."

"What I want to do," he replied, "is to show the English I can beat them at horse-riding. Although they may have Castles to live in and beds which have been occupied by Kings, we can still make more money than they can and then spend it more freely."

Salvia wished that her brother was there to answer this statement, but she thought that unfortunately he was distinctive in having lost money rather than having made it.

She was aware when they talked at dinner that Mr. Melton had made his huge fortune himself and his wife came from a family which was very rich as well.

'They may not have so much history behind them,' she thought to herself, 'but at least their pockets are filled with gold and at the moment that is more important than many other things that may be historical to those who are interested in the past, but are not very helpful to those who want to get ahead in the present.'

The conversation at dinner was most amusing and Salvia was laughing continually at all that the Americans had to say.

She was rather sorry when it was time for them to go to bed.

"Tomorrow night we will be going to a ball," the Countess announced. "In consequence we will be very late so don't get up too early tomorrow morning. However, I am sure that your son would like to ride in Rotten Row and the horses are at your disposal."

"It's real kind of you, ma'am," Mr. Melton replied. "I want to see Rotten Row again. I rode there nearly thirty years ago when I first came to England and I recall feeling inferior because all the men had such beautiful horses."

"You will find our horses are very outstanding," the Countess said. "I am sure that my daughter will show you the way and tell you all the rules that have to be obeyed by those who ride in Rotten Row."

They retired to bed early and Salvia went into her mother's room.

"They are so nice, Mama, and I think that Thomas Cooks have been very kind and sent us one of the most important families in New York. We might easily have found ourselves stuck with a far less agreeable collection."

"I will make certain that they enjoy London and at least they will meet the right people," her mother replied.

"I think you are splendid, Mama, and, if they go back home singing our praises, then we cannot really ask for more."

"I will feel guilty taking so much money if they do not enjoy themselves and meet all the right people."

"You are not to worry," Salvia told her, "and you know as well as I do that we can take them to all the most important dances I have been asked to and as long as they meet a lot of people with titles they will feel successful when they return to New York."

"It is clever of you to think of it, but I cannot help feeling that they are paying too much for too little."

"Really, Mama, that is nonsense!" she exclaimed. "What they really want is to live in a grand house which we undoubtedly have and meet grand people, of whom we know a large number."

Salvia paused before she continued,

"As the girl is pretty, I think it unlikely that she will find herself a wallflower at any ball we take her to."

"You are right, darling. But I still feel rather guilty in taking so much and being unable to give them more than we planned."

"They are quite content and you are not to worry. All you have to do is to take them to luncheon with the people I have written to and who are only too willing to welcome any friend of yours. And I will make certain that at any party we go to Mary-Lee has plenty of partners."

The Countess gave a smile.

"You have been wonderful, my darling. And I pray every night that Donald will come back soon with at least some of our money."

"I am sure that it will happen," she replied to her mother positively.

Only when she reached her own room and had said her prayers did she begin to wonder if she was being too optimistic.

She asked herself what they would do if he came back with nothing or perhaps very little of what had been stolen from him.

'Just how could he have been so foolish?' she asked herself for the one thousandth time.

Then she mused as she had done before that Donald was not the only one who had been caught by an American trap.

Unless their prayers were answered, he would be left with his pockets empty and with no one to blame but himself for the rest of his life.

*

The next day when she took Shelby and Mary-Lee to Rotten Row, they were riding her brother's best horses.

She was pleased to see that while their clothes were not the same as the English, they did not look outlandish or in any way peculiar.

Because they had been brought up, she had learnt, in the country and not in New York, they were extremely good riders. So there was no likelihood of them falling off or disgracing her in any way.

She introduced them to a number of her friends, who stopped to talk to her.

She was aware that they stared at them with interest and was sure that, as the Americans were talked about so much, they were just longing to ask her, when no one could hear, whether they were millionaires or not.

Mary-Lee looked most attractive on a horse and by the end of the hour's ride she had a number of young men asking her about America and how long she was staying in England.

"You are sure giving us our money's worth," said Shelby on the way home.

And, when Salvia smiled at him, he added,

"In fact I never knew that the English could be so friendly to strangers and have horses, which I must admit, are better than mine."

"You live and learn," Salvia said laughingly.

"That is exactly what I am doing and I have already got an entirely different conception of England than what I thought it would be like when I was at home in America."

"That is excellent and just what you should feel and I hope one day when I go to America I will feel as thrilled with New York as you are going to be with London."

"I am already thrilled with you," Shelby retorted.

She was so surprised at the compliment that for a moment Salvia could not think of an answer.

And, as they rode on, he continued,

"You are the prettiest girl I have ever seen and I don't mind telling you I've seen a good many one way and another."

"Then that is a compliment I will treasure," Salvia said. "I will pay you one back by saying that you are an experienced rider even if you don't sit on a horse in exactly the same way as we are taught to do here in England."

Shelby laughed.

"You are fishing for compliments and I will give them to you one by one so that you don't miss the honesty of them."

"Now you are flirting quite openly," she told him. "It is something I did not expect from an American. But I commend you on doing it in a very subtle manner."

Shelby laughed again.

"You are challenging me and I am just wondering how the contest will end."

"How do you expect it to end?" she asked quickly.

"I will tell you one thing which might be a surprise to you, but I rather doubt it," he continued. "It is that my mother is extremely keen that I should marry an English girl with a title."

He hesitated slightly before he went on,

"And it will make many of our friends in America envious and, as she has said so often, English women make good wives."

"I think that is indeed true," Salvia replied. "And you will have a large choice at every ball we take you to."

"I have a feeling," he grinned, "I will not have to look far away for what I am wanting."

It was quite obvious from the way he spoke what he meant.

Salvia merely touched her horse with her whip and rode more quickly so that it was difficult to have a personal conversation.

'Of one thing I am quite certain,' she told herself as she neared her home, 'and that is I have no wish, amusing as I find them, to marry an American.'

*

That night they all went to a ball given by one of Salvia's great friends, who was a Duchess and her balls were known as some of the most glamorous in the *Beau Monde*.

They always managed to engage a better band than anyone else.

The huge ballroom was decorated with flowers that made it look lovely even apart from the beautifully dressed and elegant girls who Salvia introduced Shelby to.

As the evening drew on, she could see that he was dancing rather faster and holding his partner closer than the majority of Englishmen held their partners.

But the girls seemed to like it and, when they drove back home, Shelby said that he had had six invitations to luncheon with the new friends he had made at the ball.

He had also received eight invitations to balls that were taking place this month and the next.

"That is an achievement in itself," Salvia observed.

The Countess never stayed for more than an hour at any of the balls and then she left to go home to bed.

"I am too old to stay up late," she claimed. "As you know the doctors said that I am not to exert myself in any way."

"But, of course, you must go to bed, Mama," Salvia agreed, "and I will look after our party."

She found after the very first night that the family of Americans were capable of looking after themselves.

The fourth night when they went out to a party, she took Mary-Lee home after finding her father asleep in one of the smoking rooms.

She left Shelby to find his own way home later.

He certainly managed to flirt, she thought, in a way that intrigued the English girls and was appreciated by their older sisters and even their mothers.

His compliments were usually very broad and yet he said them in such a charming manner and with such a note of sincerity that most women were only too eager to hear not one but half a dozen, if he was prepared to give them.

"There is one thing we can be quite sure about," Salvia said to her mother, "and that is our guest, Shelby, is being a great success amongst the *debutantes*."

She laughed before she added,

"What does surprise me is that even their parents are prepared to smile at him and not be affronted in any way by his compliments that are certainly overwhelming."

The Countess laughed.

"I think, my darling, it is not only the compliments which delight the parents of the young dancers. I made it quite clear that the Meltons are exceedingly rich and even the Americans admire them greatly for being in the top ten list of millionaires."

"That was clever of you, Mama. I never expected you to be so helpful. But, of course, if they are very rich everyone is prepared to be friendly and entertain them."

"Exactly," the Countess agreed. "Actually it is no lie because Mr. Melton told me only last night that he is considered one of the richest men in New York and, as you and I are aware, that is saying a great deal."

"Just why are they so rich when we are so poor?" Salvia asked.

"I think a great number of people have asked that question, but they certainly have a knack of turning copper into silver and silver into gold. As your father used to say, that is a conjuring trick which every man tries to perform, but so many fail."

"Not when they are American, although I suppose that there are some who we might be sorry for."

"From all that I have heard," her mother replied, "the streets of New York are paved with gold and every man who has any intelligence at all is a millionaire."

"That is something the English might try to do, but I doubt if they would ever be successful."

She then thought about her brother and gave a deep sigh.

Surely by now he would have found Walter, but, if he had not, the sky ahead of them was very dark.

*

The next day she had a shock when they arrived at the ball that she and her mother had been invited to when they had asked if they could bring their American friends.

As the rumour had gone round that the Americans were very charming and very rich, their hostess was only too pleased to say that she would welcome them.

The house where they were giving the ball was not far from their own.

It was to be a very grand occasion with the Prince of Wales present.

Salvia decided to wear one of her prettiest and most expensive dresses.

She was glad to notice that Mary-Lee's dress was almost as pretty as her own.

She had already learnt that Mrs. Melton had been sensible enough to find a French shop in New York where the dresses came from Paris. They were in consequence far more attractive and naturally far more expensive than those designed in America.

In fact she thought, as Mary-Lee walked with her into the ballroom, that they had been particularly fortunate in finding such an attractive girl to stay with them.

Everyone was only too delighted to open the doors to the Meltons as well as to her mother and herself.

It was then as she shook hands with her host and hostess that she could see Lord Carville beyond them in the drawing room.

She had been very careful when working with him to make him believe that she was just an ordinary girl even though she was clever at helping him with his books. And, thanks to her father, an expert at translating them.

Now when she saw him talking to a very attractive older woman, she wondered whether she should run away or somehow brazen it out.

She had just decided that she would move out of sight when, because she was thinking of him, she drew his attention.

He turned towards her and saw her moving away from their host and hostess.

She was well aware that he was astonished by her appearance.

She had been so careful how she was dressed when she went to him every morning.

She had learnt when she was working with him that he had a great many connections with different businesses in which he had been asked to either help them on the road to success or to advise them.

It was then when he left her for an appointment that she would hurry home and help with a luncheon party or travel with the Americans to where they had been invited.

But she invariably had to finish her work when she returned home and found it easier to let her mother give their guests tea while she worked in her sitting room.

At any rate his Lordship had been delighted with what she had done.

They had nearly finished his book on France and were already talking of what would have to be done with the one on Italy.

Now she saw Lord Carville gazing at her.

She realised that he was seeing her for the first time without her glasses and without the dull black clothes that she wore when she was in his house.

She was in fact wearing one of the prettiest gowns her mother had bought her before she went into mourning.

It was a soft pink with roses decorating it round the neck and waist and the fullness of the skirt.

And she had the same type of roses in her hair.

Tonight she had her mother's pearl necklace round her neck because the dress had rather a low *décolleté*.

As she saw Lord Carville staring at her, she wanted to run away and hide. Yet she told herself that it would be a very stupid thing to do.

If he had not been aware by this time that she was a lady and not just a secretary, it would be just impossible to deceive him for ever.

She turned away and spoke to the nearest person she knew.

He was a young man who was continually asking her for a dance, but, because she thought him rather dull, she invariably said she was too booked up.

Now he stood looking at her with what she thought were adoring eyes and saying as he had often said before,

"You are the most beautiful girl here and, if you do not give me a dance tonight, I swear I will go out and shoot myself."

"That would be a very stupid thing to do," Salvia said as she had said before. "If there is one thing I dislike it is men who get shot in a duel rather than shooting their opponent."

He laughed.

Then just as Salvia thought, as she had her back to Lord Carville she might be able to move away, she found him beside her.

"This is a great surprise, Miss More," he began. "I did not expect to find you here tonight."

"I am sorry if I gave you a shock," Salvia replied. "But actually I have known our hostess for years and she insisted that I should come to her party."

"You look very different from the way you look when you are working," Lord Carville remarked. "At the same time it is how I would always expect you to be."

Salvia looked at him with a twinkle in her eyes.

"I don't believe that," she said.

"I am not a complete fool. I know that the glasses you wear over your eyes are quite unnecessary and I was aware too that you are by no means an ordinary secretary. In fact I have often asked myself why you are hiding and who from."

Salvia laughed.

"That is another story. It is far too long to tell you here."

"Very well," he replied, "if we cannot talk we must dance together."

As the music began he put his arm around her waist and she then found herself moving beside him on the dance floor before she could think of a reason for not doing so.

One thing she had not expected was that he danced extremely well.

They then waltzed around the ballroom in silence and anyway, it would have been difficult to talk with the band playing.

It was only when the dance ended that Salvia found herself, almost before she could think about it, being taken into the garden.

The trees had been decorated with balloons and the flower beds had fairy lights in all of them.

It was very romantic.

In fact very lovely.

For a moment Salvia forgot that she had deceived Lord Carville and now she was having to face the truth.

Almost before she was aware of it, he had moved her through the trees and found a garden seat which was empty.

She wanted to run away, but somehow she found herself sitting down beside him.

"Now," he said, "suppose we introduce ourselves and you tell me truthfully who you are."

# CHAPTER FOUR

There was a silence while Salvia thought frantically what she could say.

Then after a moment he declared,

"Do you realise you did not give me your address? I wanted to get in touch with you after you had left this afternoon and found that no one knew where you had come from or where you had gone to."

"Why did you want me, my Lord?"

"Because something important has happened which I want to discuss with you," he replied.

She looked at him in surprise.

"What is important?"

"Well, it is somewhat more important than finding that you are here when I least expected it and looking, may I say, very lovely and so different from the woman who is helping me with my books."

Salvia laughed.

"But you can hardly expect me to come to work for you wearing an evening dress. As a matter of fact our hostess has always been very good to me ever since I was a child."

She thought that this was a good explanation as to why she was at the ball.

But she was well aware that her dress was hardly the sort to be worn by a secretary.

There was silence for a while and then Salvia said,

"Why did you want me this evening? Has anything bad happened?"

"Not exactly bad," he replied. "But I have had a proposition that I need your help with. When I was anxious to find you, I discovered that I had no idea where you lived."

"I do not think that is essential as long as I arrive on time in the morning," Salvia answered. "If I am unable to come because I am ill or something like that, I will send a messenger to tell you so."

"Now you are being difficult," Lord Carville said. "But I really need your help and I will be very upset if you refuse to do what I need."

"What is it you need, my Lord?" Salvia asked.

She was wondering just what it could be and she could not imagine any situation where he would need her presence or her help.

As if he thought that it was more significant to tell her why he needed her than to go on being astonished by her appearance, Lord Carville explained,

"After you had left a man came from the French Embassy to inform me that the Emperor of France was extremely anxious that I should go to Paris and speak at a Conference he is having with the neighbours of France."

Salvia was listening intently and he continued,

"It is an extremely important meeting and, as I have visited all the countries concerned, he thought I would be a great help not only to him but to the visiting officials who would like to hear my opinion on how Europe as a whole is progressing in this day and age."

Salvia smiled.

"That is certainly a compliment. I am sure you will be able to give them a fantastically good speech which they will go home and remember for the rest of their lives."

"You are flattering me," Lord Carville said. "But I am perfectly prepared to do what the Emperor requires. Of course with your assistance."

Salvia stared at him.

"I don't understand, my Lord."

"What I am saying is that I will be leaving for Paris tomorrow and I want you to come with me."

Salvia drew in her breath.

"I don't think that I can do it," she answered him.

"But you have to," Lord Carville insisted. "Your knowledge of Paris is fantastic and so is your knowledge of Italy and I expect that there are other countries you are also familiar with."

He smiled as he added,

"As this speech has to be really good and is also to be recorded in the books I am writing, who could do it better than you?"

Salvia took a deep breath.

She was wondering what her mother would say.

Actually if Lord Carville knew who she was, he would be well aware that it would be totally impossible for her as a Society figure and unmarried to accompany him unchaperoned.

Because she did not speak Lord Carville persisted,

"You must understand this is very significant. Not only that we would be polite and ready to help the French at this particular moment, but you do see it is everything I want to put into my book."

He paused before he went on,

"What you have told me, I would say not only to the French but to every other country. It is an opportunity that may never occur again."

He said it with a sincerity in his voice that made Salvia understand how much this meant to him.

He was in fact finding it a great compliment that, of all the people they might have asked to speak on such an occasion, they had turned instinctively to him.

Then, as she thought it over, she realised that she could stay in the background.

If Lord Carville just said that he was bringing his secretary with him, they would consider her of little more status than his valet.

All the same it was wrong and would undoubtedly upset her mother.

'I cannot do it,' she thought. 'In fact I must not.'

Lord Carville, as if he was aware of the conflict in her mind, then pointed out,

"As you work for me, I presume you are in need of money. Well, let me tell you that they have offered to pay me a large sum of money, in fact one thousand pounds for making the speech and my expenses in travelling there."

He checked himself before he went on,

"As you already know, I am a rich man and I am therefore prepared to take the one thousand pounds which they have offered me, which I had intended to refuse, and give it to you."

Salvia gasped.

One thousand pounds would make a really huge difference to the worry that her mother was experiencing at the moment.

It would also make certain they could pay everyone in the country as well as those they employed in London.

"I cannot think of anything else I can say to you, Miss More, to persuade you to make up your mind to come with me."

Salvia did not speak and he continued,

"I can only beg of you to appreciate that you are very necessary to me and so I have no wish to go without you."

Salvia drew in her breath and then she said,

"Very well, I will come with you. But I can only hope that I will be able to help you as you seem to think I will be able to do."

"Of course you will help me," Lord Carville said. "I will rely on you to make sure that what I am saying is understood by those listening and you are the one person I think who will be knowledgeable enough to know what the people present are thinking even if they keep their mouths shut."

Salvia laughed because she could not help it.

"It sounds incredibly difficult, but I suppose that I must think not only of myself but of France and, of course, anyone connected with that delightful country."

"I thought you would understand how important it is," Lord Carville replied.

He smiled at her before he went on,

"In point of fact I was told confidentially that the Emperor was annoyed and upset that Queen Victoria had paid so little attention to him and, if I refuse this invitation, it will be yet another obstacle between the English and the French, which I know that Queen Victoria has been trying to remove."

"As I have just said, I will come with you," Salvia stated. "But you must not mention to anyone here that I am doing so because my family might well be shocked at my travelling alone with you unchaperoned and refuse to let me go."

"Would you like me to speak to your family about it?" Lord Carville asked.

"No, of course not," she answered him hurriedly. "That will only make things worse. I will merely say that I am visiting some friends in another part of the country and make no mention of my going abroad."

She was speaking more to herself than to him.

After a moment, he suggested

"I think really you should tell the truth, but if that is likely to prevent you from accompanying me, then let's be secretive to everyone including your family."

He paused for a moment before he added,

"Actually I think it is best to wait until I have made my speech and talked with the guests of the Emperor so that

I do not have English Diplomats telling me what to say or making things worse than they are already."

"That is wise," Salvia agreed. "As you know the French are very touchy and they can get upset and become hysterical about anything which concerns their security and their reputation abroad."

"That is true," he admitted. "I am delighted that you will come with me, but we have to leave fairly early in the morning if we are to reach Paris tomorrow night."

Salvia did not speak and he continued,

The Conference takes place the next day and I think that I will be speaking sometime late on in the afternoon, but we will be expected to attend the Conference all day."

Salvia thought that it sounded very hard work, but she did not say so.

She was worried that her mother would be very shocked at her going even though she was disguised and Lord Carville had no idea that she was not the secretary she pretended to be.

She saw him glance again at her dress and, as if he had asked the question, she said,

"Our hostess has always been so extremely kind to me. I am not going to give you three guesses as to where my dress came from."

"I don't want to embarrass you by asking awkward questions," he replied. "But it is indeed very different from the black clothes you work in."

"I am hardly likely to wear a dress like this when I am taking down dictation," Salvia laughed.

Then with a twinkle in her eye she added,

"So I must not prevent you from dancing with the beautiful ladies whom I am sure are waiting anxiously for your invitation. I will go home very soon and start packing what I will need for Paris."

There was a quiet moment's silence and then Lord Carville said,

"May I make a suggestion?"

"Of course," Salvia replied wondering what he was going to say.

"You look just fantastic tonight. In fact to put it honestly, you are beautiful. I think that the French would prefer you looking as you do now and not how you dress when we are working and have no audience."

Salvia chuckled.

"And we certainly don't want anybody to criticise what you have written until your book is finished."

"That is true," Lord Carville agreed. "Therefore I think it will be very depressing for you to be ignored by the French, who love women to look as smart and as beautiful as you look tonight."

"Are you really suggesting that I will have time to flirt with the French when I am taking down everything you say and perhaps some of the other speeches we have to listen to which will be worth recording," she asked.

"I still want you to look a credit to English beauty and English taste."

Salvia thought that this was dangerous.

At the same time it would be difficult to refuse to do what he wanted.

So she merely said,

"My wardrobe is fairly limited, but I will see if I can please you and, of course, the French, who as I am well aware are very critical."

"I will be most disappointed if you come wearing those black working clothes," Lord Carville asserted. "If you shine there as you are doing now amongst so many attractive women, you can then hardly insult the French by dressing down to them, which I suspect you had intended to do."

Salvia thought that he was being too clever.

If she was not careful he would find out who she was.

She therefore started to question him on what he intended to say to the French.

As it was running through his mind and he was in fact rather worried about it, he was pleased to be able to talk to her as he would not have been able to talk to anyone else.

They sat in the quiet part of the garden for over an hour.

Then Salvia suggested,

"I think you should go back and dance with your hostess and her daughter. I am sure that there are a great number of other attractive young women here looking for you."

"I suppose that it would be polite," he agreed, "but I would much rather stay here and talk to you."

"We will have plenty of time tomorrow morning on the voyage to work out what it will be best to say," Salvia said, "and I think some of the notes we have already made in your book will be helpful."

"Of course they will."

Salvia rose to her feet.

"Now please," she begged, "don't say a single word to anyone here that you are taking me with you to France. Because I am a friend of the family I am sure they would be shocked to hear that I was going without a chaperone even though I am only your secretary."

"I understand," Lord Carville replied. "And thank you a million times for agreeing that you will come with me."

He paused before he went on,

"It is so vital, as I have already said, that I make a success of it. I am sure that I am not going to be able to do so unless you help me."

"Then you make it impossible for me to say 'no' and I suppose that I should say 'thank you' for giving me the opportunity, my Lord."

"But it is I who want to thank you," Lord Carville replied. "Because I know that you will not allow me to say the wrong thing. So we have to try hard to uphold Great Britain and make the French realise just how significant we are."

"Just a small job!" Salvia laughed teasingly.

Then, before he could stop her, she moved swiftly away and reached the house without seeing anyone who she knew.

She went to the cloakroom and found her cloak.

Then she said to the woman there who was one of the staff,

"Will you tell Her Grace that I am terribly sorry I have to go home to see my mother, who is not at all well? As you very likely know, she left early tonight."

"I'm sure she'd want you to go on dancin'," the woman who Salvia had often seen before said.

"My mother is more important than any ball," she replied. "She has not been herself lately."

"I'm sorry about that," the woman answered. "We always look forward to seein' her Ladyship when she does come here and, if I might say so, we've all been sayin' you're one of the prettiest and best-dressed young ladies in the whole ballroom."

"Thank you. That has cheered me up and I am so sorry to go, but as you know one's mother always comes first."

"Of course, she does," the woman said, "and you're a sensible girl to realise it."

Salvia smiled at her and then she slipped away.

Her mother had sent back the carriage when she left and it was waiting outside.

Salvia drove away and then she told the coachman to take the carriage back as doubtless the Americans would be leaving later on.

She felt that her mother would be annoyed that she was not looking after them.

But she was well aware that she was on dangerous ground and Lord Carville might easily find out by accident that she was not who she pretended to be.

In which case, she told herself, however much he may beg her to accompany him, she would be unable to do so.

In fact she was wondering what her mother would say when she told her that she was going to Paris.

At the same time a thousand pounds was certainly a thousand pounds and would save them both from worrying so much until Donald returned home.

When she reached the house, the moon was shining and she felt that it looked even more beautiful at night than it did in the daytime.

She then thanked the coachman who had brought her home and said,

"I hope for your sake that the party will not stay very late. But they have a wonderful band and that in itself is irresistible."

The coachman laughed and replied,

"Well, you looks very beautiful, my Lady. Several of Her Grace's staff said your gown were the smartest on the dance floor."

"I am so glad to hear that. Goodnight, George, and thank you again."

She ran up to the front door.

The door was opened by a night-footman, who was rubbing his eyes and he had clearly been fast asleep until she arrived.

Salvia went upstairs to her bedroom.

It was only when she got into bed did she wonder if she would be brave enough to accompany Lord Carville to France as he was so anxious for her to do.

'He has no notion that I am not who I pretend to be,' she told herself hoping that it was true. 'He will be certain that I borrowed the dress that I was wearing tonight, which made me look so different from how he has seen me look every day since I began helping him with his book.'

Then she realised that if she was to shine in Paris as he wanted her to do, she would have to take some of her best clothes with her rather than the black outfit and the other black clothes that she had worn when she was in deep mourning.

'If I do take them, it will be wrong because I will not look as he wants me to look,' she thought. 'But, if I take my best clothes, it will obviously be very questionable as to why a mere secretary has such beautiful clothes and who paid for them.'

She blew out the candle by her bed.

Then thinking of her father, she asked,

'What shall I do, Papa? If you were here, it would make everything so easy. But you will realise far better than anyone else that one thousand pounds is one thousand pounds and we need it desperately."

Then she told herself that perhaps it was her father who had thought of such a subtle way of making them feel safe until Donald returned home.

Besides there was always the fear that he would not find Walter and, if he did, he might not be able to retrieve any of the money that Walter had stolen from him.

'I must go. I have to go to Paris!' she told herself. 'It is manna from Heaven that this money should come at this moment.'

She slept for a short while.

*

Then she jumped up early and started to pack her clothes.

She first chose the smarter and simpler dresses she had.

Then because it was better to take them, even if she did not wear them, than to leave them behind and be sorry, she packed some of her best dresses.

She included some of her prettier hats and decided to travel not in black but in one of her plainer dresses.

As it was a very pale blue, it would undoubtedly be noticed especially as the hat that went with it was trimmed with feathers of the same colour.

'It is how he expects me to look,' she told herself when she gazed in the mirror.

Equally she was still worried in case she somehow caused a scandal by being alone with Lord Carville and it would make her mother angry and disappointed.

She would have all her friends asking her why she had to work for his Lordship, when as a family they were known to be very well off.

'It's no use me thinking about an answer to every question,' Salvia told herself finally. 'I will just pray that everything will go smoothly and I will not cause a scandal by my behaviour or let the secret of Donald losing all our money be known to anyone.'

When finally she went up to her mother's bedroom to say 'goodbye', she was very nervous in case her mother begged her or indeed ordered her not to go to Paris.

But the Countess was feeling tired after rather a late night.

"Are you going out, darling?" she asked sleepily as Salvia kissed her.

"You remember, Mama, I am going to Paris," she said. "I hope it will only be for two or three days and it will be wise for you to tell no one where I have gone."

"Paris," her mother murmured sleepily as if she had never heard of it. "Why are you going there?"

"I am going as I have to take down the speeches that are being made at a very important meeting," Salvia answered. "Don't worry, Mama, I will be very well looked after and I will come home as quickly as I can."

"Yes, do that, darling. I will find it difficult to keep our visitors amused until you return."

"I will leave you the list of the parties that we have had them invited to," Salvia said, putting it down on the table beside the bed, "also the people we invited to dinner next Thursday."

She smiled before she added,

"I am hoping, in fact I am almost sure that I will be back by then, but they are all old friends who will, I know, do everything they can to amuse our visitors and keep them from troubling you."

She kissed her mother again and added,

"Goodbye, Mama, and remember it is a big secret that I am making one thousand pounds by going to Paris. It is the money we desperately need that will keep us from fretting for quite a long time."

"One thousand pounds," the Countess said almost beneath her breath. "I can scarcely believe that you are managing to earn so much."

"It will keep us smiling, I would hope, until Donald returns," Salvia replied. "But don't forget to pray for him, as he has a very difficult task in front of him."

She did not wait for her mother to reply, but kissed her again and hurried towards the door.

She was certain that his Lordship was thinking out the most telling points that he would make in his speech.

She felt sure he would want every word recorded in case, when the time came, he had forgotten what he had been going to say.

'This is an adventure,' she told herself, 'and I only hope that the driver of the carriage which is taking me to his Lordship's house will not tell the servants where he has picked me up.'

The butler had been very surprised when she told him that she would hire a carriage.

"It'd be just as easy, my Lady, to take our own carriage," he pointed out.

"They were very late last night," she replied, "and I think they should rest before her Ladyship plans what she wants to do today. There was some talk of her going out into the countryside."

The butler merely nodded and she continued,

"Although I think that will be too much after such a late night, it is better to let them rest now so that it will not be too exhausting for them later on."

"Your Ladyship thinks of everything," he answered admiringly. "But that's just what your father, God bless his soul, always did and why we all admired him so much and wanted to please him."

"That is why I must try to do what Papa would have done under the same circumstances."

She thought as she drove to Lord Carville's house that he would undoubtedly be curious about her family.

He would wonder how it was possible as she was only a modern young woman earning her living to look as she had last night.

She had informed his Lordship that she was a close friend of the daughter of the Duchess.

'I am trying not to lie, Papa,' she thought, knowing that her father had always hated lies and people making out to be who they were not.

All the same it was no use pretending that they did not need the money and, as she had said before, it was just manna from Heaven at this particular moment.

She thought that her father would have laughed at what she was saying.

Yet she had to please the man who was employing her.

If he wanted her to look smart and to pretend to be grander than she really was, she had to do what he wanted.

When they arrived at Lord Carville's house, it was to find that his luggage was already in the hall.

Then the butler looking at her somewhat in surprise said,

"His Lordship's just finishing his breakfast. Do you want to join him in the dining room, Miss More, or will you go to the office?"

"When are we leaving?" Salvia asked him.

"Almost immediately," came the answer. "We are just waiting for the carriage to come round and I hears you be going to his Lordship's yacht on the Embankment."

Salvia gave a cry of delight.

"I had no idea that we were going by yacht!" she exclaimed. "That is splendid."

She felt that she had been rather stupid in thinking that Lord Carville would not have a yacht.

It was obviously much the easiest way of travelling to France than any other.

"His Lordship's yacht be a real fine one," the butler said. "He's only had it a year and the one he had before were out of date and too small he reckoned."

He chuckled as he went on,

"He's always been one for doing things as fast as possible. Sometimes too fast and then it be impossible!"

He laughed at his own joke and Salvia laughed too.

Then she heard Lord Carville's steps coming to meet her.

She waited and, as he reached her, he said,

"I might have guessed that you would be punctual. Most women invariably keep me waiting. But now you are here we will leave at once as we have no idea how rough the sea might be."

He paused before he asked her,

"Are you a good sailor?"

"So far, so good, my Lord. But then it's always a mistake to boast."

Lord Carville laughed.

"That is true enough," he agreed.

While they were talking, his carriage drawn by two horses came to the front door and a footman began to take Salvia's luggage outside.

The other footmen went upstairs and came down each with large cases.

"It looks as if we are going to spend a long time in France," Salvia remarked to Lord Carville.

"I hope not, but I do dislike not having a change of clothing when I need it."

"That is very sensible," Salvia answered. "If you will forgive me I will not keep you waiting, but I have to collect a few things from the office."

She did not wait for him to reply, but ran down the corridor to where she kept her books, pens and pencils.

She put them all into a small case she had seen in the office and thought that it was what his Lordship usually took with him.

She took two notebooks which she thought would be enough to take notes at the meeting and to put down his Lordship's speech on paper.

When she hurried back with the case that contained everything she thought she would need, it was to find that the luggage had all been placed on board.

His Lordship was waiting for her.

"I am sorry to have been so long," she apologised, "but I want to have everything we would need. Unless I am mistaken both the French and the English can be very long-winded."

This made his Lordship laugh as she had intended him to do.

Then he said,

"We will soon find out, so climb into the carriage and the sooner we are on our way the better."

'It really is an adventure,' Salvia thought to herself as they sat down in the carriage.

She was then aware that His Lordship was looking at the way she was dressed.

"You are very smart," he said, "and just as I want you to look. I am wondering why you look so different from how you have looked these past days while we have been working together."

"I have the real answer to that," Salvia replied. "I have to be careful with my best clothes and no one expects a secretary to look as if she has just stepped out of Bond Street."

"That is true," Lord Carville agreed. "At the same time clothes can be deceptive and even a secretary may have reasons for hiding herself from the world outside."

Salvia thought that this conversation was a mistake and she had no wish to lie.

But then it would be disastrous if Lord Carville was really suspicious of her being not what she was pretending to be.

She therefore changed the subject by saying,

"I just wondered if you had packed any books that would be helpful to me. There was one on French history in the study, but it is very large and I have a feeling that once we arrive in Paris there would not be much time for reading."

Lord Carville smiled.

"That is true enough, I am just wondering if I do go out to dinner or am invited to anything of great import, how I would explain that my secretary is not only beautiful but dressed in the very latest fashion."

Salvia thought that this was the sort of question she was afraid that she might have to answer.

But, because she could not think of anything clever or amusing, she merely said,

"It is a mistake to worry ourselves as to what will happen until we get there. I have heard that these sort of meetings never run smoothly and, unless I am mistaken, a great number of the speeches will be exceedingly dull."

"That is one thing mine must not be," Lord Carville asserted, "and that is up to *you*."

"What is so essential," Salvia replied, "is that you remember all the interesting things we have put into your book on France."

She paused before she went on,

"It is vital that you give to everyone who listens to you something to take away in their minds and perhaps I should add in their hearts."

Lord Carville was silent for a moment.

And then he said,

"You are quite right, of course, you are right as you always are. I am just wondering now if you should give the lecture rather than me!"

"That certainly would be sensational," she retorted, "and the sort of thing the French would think was a joke. I am sure this meeting will be serious and much of the future will depend on it."

"Yes, of course, I was only teasing. I do know that, whatever people might say, the Emperor of France is right in calling this meeting and allowing the other countries to express themselves."

"And for you to represent Great Britain," Salvia said.

"It is most certainly a great compliment and quite a number of Politicians will be envious and annoyed. At the same time I think that I am more capable of saying the right thing than most of them are."

Salvia did not answer and he went on,

"As the Emperor has asked for me particularly, it would be impossible for either them or me to refuse."

"Of course," she agreed. "Actually all the research we have done up to now will help you and as you know we have to be careful where Russia is concerned."

"If you ask me," Lord Carville replied, "Germany is becoming too big for its boots and it was Bismarck who took over all the little Principalities, which has made them far larger and more powerful than they were in the past."

There was silence for a moment.

And then Salvia said,

"I heard, although it might well not be true, that the Russians are extremely annoyed at Germany having made themselves so powerful and they want to do the same thing by taking over many of the Principalities in the Balkans."

"And so enable them to reach the Mediterranean," Lord Carville added. "Let me tell you that it is something Her Majesty will fight against and stop in every possible way as she told me when I visited her last month."

"That is good news. We don't want Germany to be too big or too strong. One thing is quite certain though is that we English have no wish to fight with the Germans."

"I hope it is something that we will never do," Lord Carville replied. "But unfortunately we cannot write the history of the future as we can write on what is happening today."

"That is very true," Salvia agreed. "But you are not to frighten me with what might happen because it is always a mistake to be afraid until it actually does."

Lord Carville laughed.

"You have the answer to everything," he said. "I think we will have plenty to laugh at when this meeting is taking place and even more when we sum it all up at the end."

"Why do you say that?" Salvia asked.

"Because most meetings of this sort are either to frighten off one's enemies or to make people think that you are stronger than you actually are."

"That is such a very good remark, my Lord, and one which will undoubtedly go into your book."

"If you are now going to put everything I say into a book," Lord Carville teased her, "we will doubtless fill the library and have to build another one in my house in the country!"

"Is your country house impressive?" Salvia asked him.

She thought that if he knew which house belonged to her family he would be very envious.

No one had seen the house in Oxfordshire without saying,

'it is the most marvellous house I have ever seen and you must be proud that it has managed to remain here for so many years without crumbling to pieces.'

The treasures in it, which had been collected down the centuries were unique, and her father had been very proud of what he possessed.

He was only curious about other people's houses because he was certain that his collection of pictures and furniture was, without any question, the best in the whole of England.

'One day when Lord Carville learns who I really am,' Salvia thought, 'he will know exactly why I am so knowledgeable on pictures, furniture and all other emblems of our glorious past.'

Equally she was certain that his collection, although she had only seen the London part of it, was outstanding and impressive.

This was because he had taken the trouble to be so knowledgeable himself and to appreciate, as many people had, what had descended down the centuries and was still in private possession.

All these things went through her mind while Lord Carville was talking about England and what England had given to the world.

"The French have had some outstanding painters," he said, "but I daresay it is one of the things that Germans envy. Yet many of our collections are unique and I think that our treasures go back in time further than many other countries."

"Of course, they do, my Lord, you can see them in the British Museum and in many country houses. I have often thought they should all be open to the public, so that we as a people can realise how precious the treasures are whoever they are owned by, is something that everyone in our country can be very proud of."

"You are quite right," Lord Carville replied. "But I thought that only I had reasoned it out."

He smiled before he added,

"I might have guessed that you had done it first."

"I think that many of the things you have already put down in your book are unique and, when you have finished it in three languages, you are, of course, planning in your mind what you will say about your own country."

"How do you know that?" Lord Carville questioned her in surprise.

"I guessed it, my Lord, but sometimes when you do speak about England you look different from when you speak about France or Italy."

"You are very observant," he praised her. "But, of course, I am indeed very proud of my own country and I am determined to make it greater than it is already."

"I am quite certain that Her Majesty will be only too willing to help you," Salvia replied. "My father has often said that despite her love for her husband, who was of course a foreigner, she is making Great Britain the most powerful country in the world."

As Salvia spoke, she realised that she had made a mistake in referring to her father.

If Lord Carville quizzed her about him, she might have to lie.

It was therefore fortunate at that moment they were on the Embankment and she was able to say,

"Oh, there are quite a number of ships on the river, and I am looking for your yacht. Have you had it a long time, my Lord?"

"Only about a year. The old one which belonged to my father was completely out of date, but I have tried to make this one as advanced as possible."

He paused before he added,

"In fact the man who built it complained that I was asking too much of him and it was impossible for me to have anything which could move so fast or be so advanced both inside and out."

Salvia laughed.

"I should have guessed that your Lordship would feel that was what you wanted. But it is extraordinary how ships have improved in the last year or two and we are no longer, as a nation, afraid of losing our superiority on the sea."

"How do you know all this?" Lord Carville asked. "You cannot, at your age, have done so much or have met so many people."

"I have been most fortunate in what I read," Salvia answered, "and that teaches me more than the people I meet."

"Well, now you are going to meet some of the best people Europe possesses. I will be interested to know what you have learnt from them when this particular meeting is over."

"I am quite certain that they will learn a great deal from you," Salvia replied.

"I hope you are right. I am depending on you to tell me exactly where I go wrong, if I do, or just what I am missing."

"I will do my best," Salvia promised him.

It was then that they boarded the yacht.

As *The Seaspray* then moved gradually out into the River Thames, Salvia thought to herself that the future was more exciting than she had ever expected it to be.

'I am really on my way to Paris, Papa,' she said in her heart, 'and you have to help me to make Lord Carville show the French, the Italians and everyone at the meeting that the English are indeed better and stronger than any of them.'

She smiled to herself as she added,

'If it is a question of who actually rules the world, they will have to face the fact that it is Queen Victoria who is supreme in Windsor Castle.'

# CHAPTER FIVE

When they sat down to dinner, Salvia thought that they might well have been dining in her mother's house or perhaps in Lord Carville's.

He had changed into his evening clothes.

And she had put on, after a little hesitation, one of the pretty evening dresses she had with her.

She thought maybe, as his secretary, that she would seem over-dressed.

She was careful not to put on one of her necklaces or her diamond earrings.

'I must try to look the part,' she thought. 'At the same time I must impress the French, otherwise I will be left alone while his Lordship goes to all the parties!'

She was quite sure, knowing the French, that they would not be hosting this spectacular meeting with all the other countries unless there was a huge amount of eating, drinking and laughter before they settled themselves down to serious business.

It was very fascinating for her to take part in it.

Equally she had to remember all the time that she was a paid servant even if a somewhat superior one.

And she must not behave in any other way as far as his Lordship was concerned.

At dinner they talked of the history of the countries who would be present and to her delight Salvia found that she knew as much as Lord Carville.

And because of her father at times she knew more.

She enjoyed what she thought was a battle of their brains.

She deliberately argued with him on certain points which she saw surprised him as they were known only to the top people concerned with the law of the country that they were talking about.

Anyhow it was an amusing dinner and she enjoyed every moment of it.

When she went to her cabin, Lord Carville said,

"I do hope you sleep well and I suppose we should breakfast early so as not to miss anything that might be happening until we know exactly where we come in on the great show."

"I am sure, as you represent Great Britain, you will be wanted all day long," Salvia said. "So we must prepare ourselves to do a great deal of hard work however tempting Paris may be."

"Tempting," he repeated. "That is a strange word for you to use."

"I do not mean it in the way you are translating it," Salvia pointed out. "I am merely thinking that if we have a lot of work concerned with what you say and what replies you receive from the other countries, I will have a great deal to write down."

She smiled as she added,

"I will, of course, have to translate from my rather unreadable shorthand into English that will read well when you take it back to England to impress the Prime Minister and the Secretary of State for Foreign Affairs."

"I have to admit that they are both delighted that I have agreed to take part in this extraordinary and unusual Conference," Lord Carville told her.

He laughed as he observed,

"I only hope that I will get a word in edgeways!"

Now Salvia laughed.

"I am not afraid of you being ignorant. After all you are very prestigious and so is England when it comes to peace in Europe and I pray that we don't have to go to war again."

"I say 'amen' to that," Lord Carville replied. "I am very sure that every country, if they have any sense, feels the same."

"I think that the exception, if there is one, are the Russians," Salvia said. "Don't forget how large they are and how desperate the Czar is to reach the Mediterranean and then, of course, India."

Lord Carville sighed.

"If only people were content with what they have and not always wanting more," he commented, "the world would be a happier place."

"That is what you must put in your book," Salvia told him. "You must make them understand that peace means prosperity. War means devastation and the loss of many fine and brilliant men who will leave their families weeping at their loss."

She spoke with so much feeling in her voice that Lord Carville stared at her in surprise.

"You sound as if you have lost someone you love," he said.

There was silence for a moment and then Salvia replied,

"That happens to all of us and the moment comes when those we love have gone and we know that no one can really take their place."

She was thinking of her father as she spoke.

Then she was aware that his Lordship was thinking that she had lost a lover.

"One thing is quite certain, my Lord, we will both have to be on our best form tomorrow. Therefore we must not go on talking, but must go to bed and give our brains a good rest."

"You are quite right," Lord Carville agreed. "Your brain will be working overtime and must be at the highest possible speed if you we to catch even a quarter of what is said so that I can put it in my books and then hand it as a present to posterity."

Salvia laughed.

"The trouble with you, my Lord, is that you are too ambitious. From the way you talk I think you want to be remembered for long after you have departed from this life and you will still be influencing whole generations of those who come after you."

"Now you are making me feel just as if I was an Emperor or the General of a great Army going into battle," Lord Carville retorted.

"That is exactly what you are. Only the Army that is following you consists of one small and rather frightened woman!"

Lord Carville chuckled.

"If you are describing yourself, then you are very wrong. May I say that at the party, as I said before, you looked beautiful in your evening dress and I am sure that there is not a man in Paris who will not tell you so."

"Then I insist on having my beauty sleep at once," Salvia answered. "Otherwise with lines under my eyes and yawning from tiredness no one will look at me twice!"

She walked down the companionway as she spoke and pushed open the door of her cabin.

Everything had been put ready for her, including a nightgown lying on the bed and the curtains were drawn over the porthole.

She turned round and said,

"Goodnight, my Lord, do sleep well and remember that every word you say tomorrow must drop shining like diamonds from your lips to inspire and, of course, entrance everyone who will be listening to you."

"You are making me frightened with every word you say," he protested. "So go to bed and I am forcing myself to believe that nothing will be ever as intimidating as you are determined to make it."

He closed Salvia's door as he finished speaking and she heard him walking towards his Master cabin.

She then sat down at the dressing table and looked at her own reflection.

'Can this really be happening to me?' she asked herself. 'I cannot help feeling it is like a play on the stage at *Drury Lane* and I am honoured to have quite a large part to play."

When she finally did climb into bed, it was quite some time before she fell asleep.

\*

But, when she awoke, the sun was then pouring in through the porthole.

As the yacht was still, she guessed that they were in Port.

On Lord Carville's orders, they had sailed through the night and were now in the Port of Marseilles.

She knew from there that they would be able to take a fast train to Paris.

In fact, by the time she was dressed, his Lordship was already calling for her.

His valet was packing the few things that she had taken out of her case ready to go ashore and be put in the carriage which was to take them to the Railway Station.

It was certainly, Salvia thought, a most comfortable way of travelling rather than crossing the Channel in one of the ferries that only had one or two small private cabins on board and this meant that there was always an unseemly rush by pushy travellers to hire them.

They ate breakfast very quickly.

And then they were driven to the Railway Station where the Captain of the yacht had already sent an Officer ahead to engage their compartments.

They had two First Class compartments right next to each other.

When Salvia saw what a crowd of people there was on the train, she was very glad that everything had been arranged so smoothly for them.

She had heard that some French trains were not very comfortable at night and it was not always possible to have a compartment to oneself.

And it was then impossible to complain about the accommodation or that the train was slow.

Actually their train ran so swiftly that they reached Paris in very good time.

"We are not staying at the British Embassy as there will be quite a number of my friends there," Lord Carville said, "and I thought it might be embarrassing for you."

Salvia did not reply and he went on,

"We are therefore going to a hotel, which is reputed to be the best in Paris and we have a suite which I am sure we will find not only comfortable but where we will not be continually disturbed."

Salvia thought that this sounded very sensible of his Lordship.

She had been rather afraid that, if they had stayed at the British Embassy, there might easily have been people who would have recognised her.

And so they would be surprised that she was alone with Lord Carville, unchaperoned.

She had brought her glasses that she intended to wear when they were taking part in the Conference.

But she did recognise that it was not a particularly fool proof disguise.

She had not really thought seriously, when she had agreed to go to Paris, that she would be noticed.

At the same time there would be distinguished men from England and many had been her father's friends.

'I suppose that I should have refused to accompany him,' she told herself. 'But, of course, a thousand pounds was a temptation that I could not under the circumstances turn down.'

\*

When she jumped out of bed the next morning, she dressed herself in the plain black clothes that she had worn when she had first visited Lord Carville.

She had put them in at the last moment thinking that the other clothes she had with her were exceptionally smart.

They would undoubtedly draw attention to her even before anyone noticed her face or her eyes.

She had had so many compliments about her eyes.

"They are like sunshine," several men had said to her and one man had complimented her by saying,

"The moment you look at me I feel as if you are drawing my heart from my body and I can do nothing to stop it!"

The glasses seemed a reasonably good disguise and she thought, as she looked at herself in her black suit and her hair brushed back and as straight as she could make it, no one would take a second look at her.

She was safe from those who would undoubtedly carry back to London with them the story that she was with Lord Carville and unchaperoned.

His Lordship made no comment on her appearance.

They drove in a carriage from the hotel to the huge building where the Conference was to take place.

When they arrived, there were already a number of people passing through the big double doors.

As most of them were men, Salvia thought that she might become somewhat conspicuous, but to her relief no one seemed to notice her.

Even those who greeted Lord Carville, who were obviously English, never gave her a second glance.

She found that while he was seated on a platform, the secretaries and nearly every delegate had one with him, were beneath it on what usually would have been the first row of those listening to what was taking place.

Each secretary had a small table in front of him or her and pens, pencils and notepaper were on it.

Salvia thought that this was very well arranged.

When the representatives of each country filed onto the platform, there was loud applause from the rest of the room which was gradually filling up.

By the time the Conference started, Salvia thought that it would be impossible for anyone else to find a seat in the auditorium. Or for that matter to sit on the floor.

The Conference was opened by a Frenchman who was the equivalent of the Speaker of the British Parliament.

He received a great volume of applause when he appeared and then began welcoming the visitors from other lands.

Then he said that this was an extremely important meeting for the French because Paris was, and always had been, the centre of Europe.

And they were absolutely determined never to lose that position.

Salvia wrote down almost everything he said.

He was followed by the French Prime Minister and the Secretary of State, who more or less repeated what had already been said by the first speaker.

She was delighted when, after the French welcome to their visitors, Lord Carville representing Great Britain, was the next speaker.

He spoke, Salvia thought, exceedingly well.

He thanked the French for this magnificent display and also made it clear that England was extremely anxious that there should be no more conflicts in Europe.

That every country should work to bring peace and prosperity to its people, which to sum it all up in just one word meant 'peace'.

He spoke clearly so that everyone could hear what he said.

He looked so handsome as he did so that Salvia thought that the English should be very proud of him.

He was absolutely the right person to represent the country.

When he sat down at the end of his speech, there was great applause.

The French Master of Ceremonies thanked Lord Carville profusely for what he had said.

The Greek delegate came next and he was followed by the Italian.

By this time Salvia was beginning to feel that her fingers were aching and she wanted to rest them.

But she knew that it was her duty to take down as much as possible of what was being said.

However, she gave a deep sigh of relief when the delegates decided on an early luncheon.

But she soon realised that they were only doing so because the most significant part of the Conference would take place in the afternoon.

If the luncheon was well arranged for the speakers, the secretaries were not so fortunate.

They had to collect what they wanted to eat from a bar and there was very little choice and, although there was white wine and non-alcoholic drinks, there was not much variety.

Nor was the quality what one would expect from the French.

When they went back to the Conference, she was beginning to feel that her fingers were still aching and she longed for a breath of fresh air.

But there was no time to go out even for just a few minutes.

Again she was scribbling down all that was being said by yet another speaker who, apart from talking almost incoherently, became very short of breath.

He turned out to be another speaker from Germany and, as she had already written down the first one, she did not bother with this one as it all sounded very similar.

Then, to her delight, Lord Carville spoke again.

This time he spoke about a great many of the things that he had put in his book.

His call for peace was so compelling and so well delivered that he was given a huge roar of applause from those listening.

There were two other speakers.

Then a French delegate closed the meeting and said that they would all be back again tomorrow morning.

He thanked those who had shown such enthusiasm for peace and prosperity which they were all seeking.

Although there was a crowd making for the doors, Salvia found herself, sooner than she had expected, driving back alone with Lord Carville to their hotel.

"Are you exhausted?" he asked Salvia.

"My fingers, I think, no longer belong to me," she replied. "But I must congratulate you on your speech, my Lord, I think it was brilliant."

"I think you have to congratulate yourself," Lord Carville said. "After all I was only saying a great number of things that you told me to say in the book I am writing about France."

"You were splendid," Salvia said, "and I must be careful not to forget the new ideas you put in, which are not in the original volume."

"I think you inspire me," Lord Carville told her. "I am sure that we must both relax now before we start again tomorrow."

"I agree," Salvia answered.

"I thought you would. I therefore refused several invitations for dinner tonight. I thought we would have an excellent meal at a place where I always dine when I come to Paris."

He laughed as he added,

"I doubt if afterwards you would want to go to the theatre or even more exhausting to a dance."

"I think, if I have a good dinner, all I will want is to go to bed. I found some of the speakers difficult to follow and as I have said my fingers are so stiff that I feel they are almost paralysed."

"They will be a lot better tomorrow," Lord Carville answered encouragingly. "Now what I am certain that we both want is a hot bath followed by a glass of champagne before we go out to dinner."

Salvia smiled at him.

"I certainly agree to that," she enthused.

She went to her own room and had a very pleasant bath before she put on one of the pretty dresses that she had brought with her.

When she then entered the sitting room where his Lordship was waiting for her, she saw him gazing at her.

He was certainly admiring her appearance, although he did not say so.

He only rose to his feet and then put a large glass of champagne in her hand.

"This is one of the best champagnes France has ever produced," he said. "I am sure you will enjoy it."

"I am enjoying it," Salvia replied. "You must tell me what you are planning to say tomorrow, my Lord."

Lord Carville held up his hands.

"Tomorrow has not yet arrived. I have had enough today to last me for a long time. Let's talk of other things and, more important than anything else, ourselves."

Salvia smiled at him.

"I would indeed enjoy it," she answered.

"I thought you would say that," he replied. "Now come along and I know you will find the place where we are dining, which is undoubtedly the best in Paris, exactly what we both need at this very moment."

Salvia felt later that she had been optimistic enough to think that he was predicting what would really happen.

Unfortunately when they entered the restaurant that was exclusive and attractive and already almost full, there were several people present who knew him.

They were French and while he kissed the women's eagerly outstretched hands, she knew that what she hoped would be a *tête-à-tête* that evening was not going to take place.

She was introduced to a party and they were cajoled into joining Lord Carville's friends who were so obviously part of the Social world of Paris.

The men paid her compliments, but she was very much aware that one of the women was flirting with Lord Carville.

She was whispering secrets in his ear which only he could hear.

The conversation Salvia had was, as she had known in the past, a mixture of very exaggerated compliments and questions of curiosity.

There were statements that only Frenchmen could make about the world in general.

She made those talking to her laugh and she was thankful that her French was so good that they never once said that they could not understand what she was trying to say.

But she could not help being very aware that Lord Carville's eyes were twinkling.

The attractive Frenchwoman was whispering most of the things she wanted to say so that it was impossible for anyone else to hear them.

The dinner was really delicious but somewhat long-winded.

Salvia knew that she was tired and anxious to go to bed.

It was, however, well after midnight when the party broke up and she then heard the Frenchwoman say to Lord Carville,

"We will meet tomorrow night, my dear Ivan, and I will be looking forward to it."

Lord Carville kissed her hand.

As he did so, she bent forward and kissed him on his cheek.

Then they walked towards the carriages which were waiting for them outside.

"Until tomorrow and may the hours pass quickly," Salvia heard the woman saying in her attractive Parisian French to Lord Carville.

Salvia climbed into the carriage.

Then she waited several minutes as he once again said 'goodbye' to his friends.

As he joined her, they drove off towards their hotel.

"I hope you did not mind," Lord Carville said, "but, as I had to explain why you were with me and I told my friends that you were a relation of my mother's and, as you were so keen on politics and were engaged to a Politician in England, you had come with me to learn what would be useful to you in the future."

For a moment Salvia was so surprised at what he was saying that she did not answer.

Then she thought that he had made a great mistake, as he had admitted that they were there alone together in Paris.

It would, of course, if the story did reach London, give her a very bad reputation which would definitely upset her mother a great deal.

"I am sure you were right to have said that," she answered. "But I think tomorrow night I had better stay in the hotel."

"I cannot allow you to do so," he replied.

"I will be all right," she assured him. "And it will give me a chance to get down more of what was said than I could put down when they were actually saying it."

There was silence for a moment.

Then Lord Carville said,

"It was difficult for me to say that I had no wish to join them for tomorrow night. But actually I would much rather we were alone and had a good chance of resting after what will undoubtedly be a very tiring day."

"But, of course, you must see your friends," Salvia said. "I am sure that they will have a great deal to say which might be very useful to you. You have to know the French point of view before you can either disapprove or adjust it. Your friends would think it strange if you came to Paris and then neglected them."

"We will see tomorrow night," Lord Carville said, "but my feeling at the moment is that quite frankly I would much rather be at the hotel with you."

"You cannot talk business for all of the night," she replied. "I think the main thing tomorrow night will be to forget for a moment what has already been said and what is still left to be said."

Lord Carville laughed.

"You sum it up excellently, but, as I have already said, I have no wish to be with my friends tomorrow. But I could hardly refuse to join them without making them very suspicious as to why we were here together."

"I suppose that is inevitable," she said with a sigh. "The French invariably think the worst if they see a man and a woman alone together!"

"My father used to say," he responded, "that to an Italian all roads lead to Rome and to a Frenchman all roads lead to bed!"

Salvia chuckled.

"I do think that sums it up completely," she replied. "So you and I must not be seen alone together while we are in Paris."

"I can think of an answer to that," Lord Carville said slowly. "But I will tell you what it is tomorrow."

They returned to the hotel and said 'goodnight' and then Salvia went to her room.

She admitted to feeling very tired.

As she recognised, it was because she had had to concentrate so intently on what she was taking down and actually it was something that she had never done before.

When she had climbed into bed, she thought of how well Lord Carville had spoken.

Also the way that the Frenchwoman had kissed him when he had raised her hand to his lips.

'I suppose she is an old flame,' Salvia thought to herself. 'I must be tactful in keeping out of the way.'

It was, however, easier said than done.

The next morning while they were having breakfast in their private sitting room, a letter was handed in for Lord Carville.

He opened it and declared,

"I might have guessed that this would happen. It is an invitation from two of my friends we met last night to dine at their house after the Conference has ended instead of eating at a restaurant."

He was looking down at the letter as he spoke.

After a moment's pause Salvia said,

"I am quite certain that the invitation is for you, my Lord, and not for me."

"Actually, that is the truth," Lord Carville replied, "and I will refuse it or if you agree I will suggest that you come with me."

Salvia shook her head.

"You know as well as I do that the pretty lady you were flirting with last night will want you alone. However close a relative I might pretend to be, she does not want me."

"I have already said," Lord Carville repeated, "that I will refuse the invitation because I thought that it might amuse you if we went to one of the shows while we are here."

Salvia did not speak and he went on,

"They are always rather amusing if perhaps a little risqué. But, if we have a box and sit so that no one below can see you clearly, we will see Paris as everyone expects it to be."

Salvia smiled.

"That is a very clever idea of yours! But I am sure that you would rather be alone with the beautiful lady who was whispering to you most of the way through dinner."

She paused and Lord Carville parried,

"You have told me to understand the French to the best of my ability and that, in fact, is exactly how I expect a Frenchwoman, who has such a lurid reputation as Yvette, to behave."

Salvia raised her eyebrows.

"Has she a bad reputation?"

"Well, most certainly London would think so. But in France she is allowed to be as alluring as she wants to be and a great number of men have found her irresistible."

"Is that how you find her?" Salvia asked before she could prevent herself from doing so.

Then she blushed and added,

"Forgive me! I had no right to ask that question. It must be the French air which is affecting me, which as we both know affects everyone who comes to Paris."

"How old are you?" Lord Carville then asked her unexpectedly.

Because she had never anticipated him asking such a question, Salvia told him the truth.

"I am twenty," she replied.

"But you are so clever and have astounded me with your knowledge of history. But I feel you know very little about love or the flirtations which so many women think of as their right and have no wish for any other conversation."

Salvia felt herself about to blush and so she replied,

"What you are really saying, my Lord, is that I am very ignorant and perhaps that is the truth. I have spent a great deal of time in the country riding and being happy with my dogs and my family."

She paused before she went on,

"I suppose I have travelled a great deal. But I have never come into contact with the older French women such as those we met last night."

"I am sure that is the truth," Lord Carville replied. "Yet when you told me you had been to so many countries I somehow imagined that you were grown up when you did so. But now I think about it I did not realise you were so young or so inexperienced in love which is all most women think about."

"I am sure that is unkind," Salvia said. "The women I have met, although I admit they are either much older, like my mother's friends or about my age, don't know how to flirt and the men I have met were, of course, English and did not know how to anyway!"

Lord Carville laughed.

"I am sure *that* is unfair. But I know exactly what you mean. I suppose it was quite wrong of me to bring you here and I apologise."

He gazed at her before he continued,

"But then I thought you were much older simply because you spoke as if you were and I could not believe a young girl would have gained such an amazing knowledge of history and the European countries unless she was very much older than you appear to be."

"What you are really saying to me is that I am very ignorant." Salvia repeated. "Especially where the French are concerned."

"Nonsense!" he exclaimed. "You told me exactly what to say and it was clever of you and so brilliant that I have been thinking of it ever since I came here. I intend to put forward a great number of ideas which you gave me when I speak again tomorrow."

"That is something I am very happy to hear," Salvia replied. "It is what I want to concentrate on, so while you go out with your French friends tomorrow night, I will stay home and think of all the things you have not yet said in your speeches, but which you certainly should say before we leave."

"You put it so very nicely," he complimented her, "but let me say, and I am telling you the truth, I would rather dine with you tomorrow night and discuss what is important than waste my time and my brain in flirting quite unnecessarily in the French manner."

He paused before he emphasised,

"It means very little which is serious and is really a question of passing the time."

Salvia thought that this was too far-fetched for her to believe him.

At the same time she had no wish to quarrel over something which was not really that important and would waste what she was sure was valuable time in thinking out what he should say at the Conference.

"You must do what you think best, my Lord," she said, "and thank you for a delicious dinner."

She went to the door and then she turned back to say,

"I thought that you spoke so splendidly today and I will pray that you will speak even better and even more commanding in what you say tomorrow."

She was gone before he could reply.

He rose and went to the window and looked out into the darkness.

The moon was moving slowly up the sky.

It was some time before he went to bed.

# CHAPTER SIX

Once they had reached the meeting, Salvia thought that she would never see Lord Carville again.

There were so many private conversations between the speakers and a great number of Press wanting special and intimate answers from those in authority.

In the end she had very little to write down but a lot to listen to and watch.

When they returned to the hotel where they were staying, Lord Carville changed his clothes very quickly and said he knew that she would understand but he had to go to a dinner party given for the speakers by the Emperor and it was impossible to refuse to be present.

"Of course, you must go, my Lord."

"But I feel very guilty at leaving you here alone," he replied.

Salvia smiled.

"You must not worry about me. I will go to bed and either read the reports of what we have just been doing from the newspapers or else make notes of what you might have to answer tomorrow."

"I only hope and pray that it will not be too long," Lord Carville said.

Before Salvia could think of a suitable reply to his remark he had gone.

She had her supper alone and then got thankfully into bed.

Her hand was still aching from all the work she had done during the day.

She thought if no one else deserved a good rest, she certainly did considering that she had done more shorthand in the last two days than she had ever done in her life before.

It was, of course, what was expected of a secretary.

She knew that fundamentally she was really happy.

She was doing something exceedingly interesting instead of perhaps taking down dull household accounts or orders for the garden.

These would certainly not be as interesting as what she was doing now.

She had so enjoyed hearing the speeches, especially Lord Carville's, because she had been so involved with its preparation.

When she finally fell into a deep asleep, she dreamt that she was riding at the family house in the country.

\*

It took her a moment or two when she opened her eyes to remember where she was.

It was then that she began to think about what Lord Carville would say today, remembering that tomorrow was the last day of the Conference.

It then suddenly occurred to her that, although he had spoken in a very excellent way, he had not yet been the great success she wanted for him.

And then, as she was dressing slowly, the ideas came into her head.

She realised that what she was thinking was exactly what had been wanted previously at the other meetings.

She was already at the breakfast table when Lord Carville came in.

"Good morning," he greeted her. "I hope you had a good sleep last night which was more than I had."

"Were you very late, my Lord?"

"I did not get back here until three o'clock," he answered. "They talked and talked."

He helped himself to a dish on the sideboard and went on,

"Needless to say their talk took them nowhere and they did not say anything sensational which we had hoped someone would."

"Then that is just what I was thinking you should do," Salvia smiled.

"Well, today is my very last chance. Tomorrow we merely close with speeches from the French who organised the whole Conference and it is doubtful if I will have any time left to speak again before we return home."

"That is why today is so important," Salvia replied. "I have thought of a few things that you should say which have not already been said."

"Then you must be very clever. I thought they had covered all the ground one way or another mostly repeating what had been said before. But only twisting it round in another way."

Salvia helped herself to some more kedgeree before continuing,

"That is exactly why you must be really positive. When I was listening yesterday, I thought that no one was putting anything new forward or what had not been said before repeatedly."

Lord Carville looked across the table at her.

"What are your suggestions?" he asked.

"Well, first," Salvia said, "I want you to look at the headlines I have put on these pieces of paper. Then I will explain to you exactly what I believe is really required at this Conference."

"If you think it is something that has not been said already," Lord Carville replied, "I will be really delighted."

"I have now written down what I want you to say," Salvia told him, "if you don't think it impertinent on my part."

"You know perfectly well I would not think that if you suggested that I sing the National Anthem! You have been a tremendous help already and I quite believe, being you, that you could help me once again."

"Actually I do think that you helped yourself when you accepted what I suggested for the books that you were writing at home," Salvia pointed out.

"I have almost forgotten them."

But she knew from the smile on his lips as he spoke that this was not true.

"Very well," she began. "You remember that we tried to find the special attributes for every country which they desperately needed to make them great."

"I recall you suggesting that to me," Lord Carville replied.

"Well, this is what I suggest you say today. I have written it down to make it clearer, also in case you want to add to it."

Lord Carville read what she had written.

It took him some time and Salvia poured herself out another cup of coffee while he was doing so.

When he had finished reading it, he put the paper down on the table and exclaimed,

"The whole trouble is that you should be doing this rather than me! I suppose the day will come when women will take their place at the top of everything! Even Prime Minister!"

Salvia smiled and he carried on,

"But at the moment we are limited to men and it is quite obvious to me that you have a far deeper imagination and far more original ideas than I have or are likely to have in the future."

"Nonsense!" she cried. "I have only put down what you and I have discussed together and there are as many ideas that came from you as came from me."

"You are being very generous, but, of course, you are right and this is exactly what is needed and no one else is aware of it amongst the speakers."

Salvia smiled at him.

"Then I have really helped?"

"Of course, you have helped. You helped in a way I did not think anyone could do and I don't know how to thank you."

"You will thank me if your speech is the sensation I predict it will be," Salvia answered.

Lord Carville glanced at the clock.

"I would like to talk it over more intimately with you," he said, "but unfortunately I promised we would be at the Conference before it begins as the Chief of the whole show wants to talk to us before we start."

Salvia laughed.

"I should think that you will have enough talking without that," she remarked.

"I agree with you, but I have no wish for England to be backward in any way or to insult the French who are very touchy if one refuses anything they want."

"I can understand that," Salvia replied. "But don't forget that you must make them realise that England is the leader of Europe and not France."

Lord Carville laughed.

"It is doubtful if they will accept that, but I will do my best," he promised, "because you have asked me to do it."

"No one can say more, my Lord. Just give me time to fetch my hat and coat and then I expect the carriage will be at the door waiting for us."

"I will be very annoyed if it is not," Lord Carville answered as she ran into her bedroom.

It only took her a moment to put on the plain hat she wore when she was working and a coat that covered her dress.

Then they drove off from the hotel.

She knew by the expression on Lord Carville's face that he was considering what she had written for him and making sure that he remembered exactly in his speech all that she had suggested.

It was a short distance to where the Conference was taking place.

When they arrived, there were already a number of people in front of them alighting from their carriages.

Lord Carville walked off to the private room where he was to talk with the Chief.

Salvia went into the Conference Hall and took her place which she had occupied the previous day.

It seemed to her a long time before the speakers came out onto the platform and took their usual places.

By this time the centre of the Hall was filled with officials from every country including England.

Looking round Salvia thought that there was not an empty place in the whole auditorium.

The Chief spoke first saying how consequential this meeting had been and that he was quite sure a great deal of good would come from it.

Then he called on Lord Carville, representing Great Britain, to speak first.

He rose to his feet.

Salvia knew that his well-pronounced and excellent French would be understood by everyone present in the Conference Hall.

Then she realised that he was remembering all that she had said to him.

And she thought that coming from him it sounded very impressive.

He began by saying that the three greatest countries in Europe were here today and this was an opportunity that he had always wanted to have.

"I am going to take my own country first," he said. "I think you will all remember King George IV. He was called 'the First Gentleman of Europe'. It was something revolutionary at the time. It has since been copied by all the young men in England. It is the man himself who is important. It does not matter if he is a King or a crossing sweeper."

He paused for a moment and smiled at his audience before he went on,

"He has good manners. He looks after his wife and children and brings them up to be as good a citizen as he is himself. As he is a gentleman, he tries to help everyone who appeals to him and more than anything else to set a fine example which is becoming characteristic of the whole nation."

There were a number of murmurs in the Hall as Lord Carville carried on,

"If a man keeps his word, he is polite and helps everyone he can and when he dies they say that he was a great gentleman. That is what England has contributed to the world."

There was a short pause before he said,

"Now for France. We all love France. We know it is the one place in the world where we feel our temperature rising and we become excited the moment we set foot in Paris. Paris has a knack, which no other Capital City has, of making people begin to laugh and feel happy almost as soon as they step into it."

Everyone in the large hall was listening intently as he continued,

"Needless to say the women are the most attractive and the seductive in the whole of Europe. It is to Paris we come when we feel lonely and mournful and we go away laughing and then we become imbued with a new spirit of determination which Paris itself has given us."

There was a great murmur from the Hall at this and some delegates wanted to clap.

But Lord Carville pressed on,

"Now we come to the third great country here today which is Italy. I believe that all of us here are Christians. As Christians we believe that what we all do in this world carries us on to the next. From there I believe that those we call angels are helping us, leading us and showing us the way to make the world a better place to live in than it is at the moment."

He looked round at the audience as he went on,

"I am quite certain, as I am sure you are, that there has never been a moment in our lives yet when we have sent up a prayer to Heaven for help and it has not been answered."

He paused for a moment before he added,

"Therefore I think one of the most important things for us to do is to go out and bring all these things to the world which is so sadly in need of them."

There was a further murmur of agreement from the delegates.

Lord Carville continued,

"Especially give them God to believe in. He will help them in a way which I have no need to explain to you that they would find very different from what their religion can offer them at the moment."

He went on to speak of how the great example of their countries could help Europe as well as the rest of the outside world.

He then stressed that it was their duty to bring love, happiness and faith to everyone who needed it.

"We have been so very lucky in being born where we have. We must think of the other people who have none of the guidance, help and faith which has made us come here today because we believe that what we have we must give to those who are in need of it."

When he sat down, there was tremendous applause.

The whole Hall even rose to their feet to clap him enthusiastically.

Salvia gave a sigh of relief.

She had been afraid that he would not stir people, but he had managed to do so brilliantly.

She knew that he would always be remembered and respected for what he had said today.

When they then broke up for the audience to have something to eat, they were all talking and praising Lord Carville's address.

"It is certainly something I never expected to hear," one Frenchwoman said. "But I will always remember him and if it is a question of being a gentleman, then I will see that my sons follow his advice as soon as they are able to toddle."

'That is just what we want to hear,' Salvia thought.

As she knew that what he had said in his speech they had discussed in detail all the way to France, she felt that her father had inspired her to say the right things to Lord Carville.

No one could have put them over more positively or with more charm, which made him irresistible to the audience

It was a moment which made Salvia draw in her breath.

At the same time she was so pleased at what had happened that she felt the tears well up in her eyes.

After a number of questions had been asked and answered, the audience sat down and the next speaker rose to his feet.

There was no doubt that Lord Carville's speech had been the best speech of the day and the one that would be remembered by all present.

Salvia felt so proud that he had not questioned her contribution.

She saw that he had spoken with such sincerity that it was impossible for anyone listening to him to have failed to agree with what he was portraying.

There was a great deal more to be discussed.

But each speaker referred in some way or another to what Lord Carville had said and Salvia knew that there was no doubt that his speech would live on.

Perhaps it would be the beginning of a completely different attitude amongst the European communities than there had been before.

But she was very much aware that Russia was not represented at the Conference and they might easily be a difficult enemy in the future.

'At the least,' Salvia thought, 'Lord Carville has proposed something that has not been suggested before. If it prevented, as he had said at the end of his speech, there being any more wars, then it was a great and fruitful step in the right direction.'

Then it was only when they were driving back to the hotel later in the afternoon that Lord Carville said,

"I cannot imagine just how you were so clever as to suggest that I spoke as I did today."

Salvia smiled as he went on,

"When we had stopped for a bit to eat at midday, a representative from every country came up to tell me that they were so impressed by what I had said and they would certainly try to carry out my suggestions."

"I thought they would," she replied, "but, of course, Russia may be difficult."

"I cannot help feeling that it is more likely to be Germany. Bismarck has enlarged his country a great deal by taking possession of so many Principalities. In doing so he has made Germany greater than she has ever been in the past."

He frowned before he finished,

"Otherwise I believe that everyone wants peace and prosperity rather than lying awake at night wondering who will strike them next."

"You were really splendid, my Lord! Absolutely splendid," Salvia told him.

Then, as they neared the hotel, Lord Carville turned to Salvia,

"I have bad news for you."

"What can that be?" Salvia asked, looking at him in surprise.

"We have all been invited to dine with the Emperor again tonight," he said, "and, as I cannot take you with me, I was afraid that you would be alone."

"I can so easily go to bed early as I did last night," Salvia answered.

"No," Lord Carville replied. "I have already sent a messenger to the friends I had promised to dine with and someone will fetch you before dinner. I am sure that you will enjoy being with them."

She thought to herself that she would much rather be alone.

But before she could say so, Lord Carville added,

"I am certain that you will spend a happy evening with them or perhaps they will take you to a theatre. I only wish we could go together as we planned to do, but I do not dare offend the Emperor."

"No, of course, you must not," she agreed. "I am sure that your sensational speech has already been brought to his notice."

"I would much rather be with you," Lord Carville asserted. "But I have no choice in the matter."

"But it will be interesting for you to meet him and see if he is as charming as he is reported to be especially where beautiful ladies are concerned."

Lord Carville laughed.

"We know he has a very soft spot in that direction," he replied. "I have often wondered why the Empress does not interfere forcefully."

"Perhaps she does not know or she realises that she cannot alter the impossible."

They both laughed.

As they arrived at the hotel, Lord Carville hurried to his own room to change into his evening clothes.

Salvia had a bath and did the same.

She could not help feeling sad that they could not spend their last night in France together.

'He is so exciting to talk to,' she reflected. 'But perhaps if he had the choice he would rather be with that pretty lady who kissed him last night than with me.'

She put on an attractive evening gown, which she had brought with her.

She had just picked up her cloak when there was the sound of the door in the sitting room being opened.

Salvia wondered who it could be.

Then she found that it was the Frenchman who had been at the party last night and who she thought was rather unpleasant.

She thought that he was slightly pushy and, when he had held onto her hand to say 'goodnight', he had held it rather longer than was absolutely necessary.

She thought, although it might be her imagination, that the expression in his eyes was rather intrusive.

Now she could only say,

"*Bonsoir, monsieur*. Have you been kind enough to come and fetch me? I was just about to order a carriage."

"I have come here to take you out," the Frenchman replied, "for the simple reason that our hostess cannot offer you the entertainment she agreed to in the afternoon. She had forgotten she has a most important engagement which concerns one of her daughters. She felt certain that you would understand that under the circumstances she would not be at home."

"Of course, I understand," Salvia replied. "It is very kind of you to come to the hotel and explain to me what has happened."

"I have not come just to explain it to you," he then replied, "but to take you out to dinner. I know all the places where the food is the best in the whole of Paris, which I know you will enjoy before you go back to the rather dull menus of England."

"It is very kind of you, *monsieur*, but I will be quite happy here."

"That is something I just cannot allow nor can you refuse what your hostess from last night has arranged for you," the Frenchman persisted. "She would be very hurt and upset if she thought that her forgetfulness had caused you to dress yourself and look so pretty for nothing."

The way he spoke made it impossible, Salvia knew, for her to protest that she did not want to dine with him alone.

She therefore responded,

"I can only thank you for being so kind to me and I am sure that the French are more expert when it comes to food than any other country in Europe."

"You speak as though you have tried them all," the Frenchman remarked.

Salvia smiled.

"I have tried most of them and my father, who I travelled with, always said, 'if you want a good meal, then we must go to France'."

The Frenchman chuckled.

"Then I will be very disappointed if you do not find tonight's meal the best you have had so far and it will excel anything you have ever tasted in England."

He spoke almost scornfully.

Salvia longed to argue with him, but she thought that it would be a mistake.

She merely left the sitting room and walked down the stairs to where his carriage would be waiting.

They did not have far to go.

The restaurant, Salvia knew at a glance, was one of the best in all of Paris.

Her companion whose name she remembered with some difficulty was Monsieur Henri Girard.

He took a long time in choosing what they should order and discussing it in great detail with the owner of the restaurant until Salvia longed to say,

'Hurry up and let's have something to eat!'

Eventually the owner went off with the menu.

Monsieur Girard then turned towards her and put his hand over hers.

"You are so very lovely," he murmured. "Only the best is good enough for anyone so beautiful."

Salvia smiled and with some difficulty removed her hand.

"You must not pay me such a big compliment," she told him. "Remember in England we seldom say anything more than, 'you look all right,' or perhaps on very special occasions they say a little bit more!"

Monsieur Girard laughed.

"I am quite sure that you are called 'very beautiful' wherever you go or whatever you wear. As it is I find you enchanting and I just cannot think of a better adjective to describe you."

He was speaking in French and Salvia knew that it was no use arguing with him.

Instead she said,

"Do tell me about the Emperor as Lord Carville is dining with him again tonight. We have heard many stories about him in England and some of them are not entirely to his credit."

"I don't want to talk about our Emperor tonight," Monsieur Girard said. "I want to talk about you. You are so very lovely and should not be doing anything as dull as being a secretary to his Lordship."

"It is a job I greatly enjoy," Salvia replied, "and his speech today was really splendid."

"I would rather hear you talking than listen to him," Monsieur Girard retorted.

Salvia knew that it was the sort of remark that any French girl would accept as an inevitable compliment and of no particular value.

Then she merely asked him,

"Tell me about this restaurant. Has it been going for years or has it opened recently?"

"I am not interested in the restaurant," he answered quickly, "only in *you*. I cannot imagine, unless you are in love with his Lordship, why you should work so hard as to take down his speech and doubtless as well the speeches of the representatives of other countries."

"I find it extremely interesting. In fact I was only thinking today of how much I had learnt and how much I had enjoyed coming to Paris in a very different way from how I had been here before."

"You mean you came as a visitor?"

Salvia nodded.

"I do wish I had known you then," Monsieur Girard said. "And I could have shown you Paris as no Englishman could. I would like us to be alone so that we can get to know each other without hurrying, as I must do tonight if, as I am told, you are leaving for England tomorrow."

"As the Conference has now ended," Salvia replied, "there is no point in us staying any longer."

"I can think of one hundred reasons why you could stay," the Frenchman answered. "Of course, as they would all concern you, you should not find it too difficult to listen to them."

He was now obviously flirting with her and it was something that Salvia had no wish to happen.

"Tell me about yourself," she suggested. "Are you a bachelor or married to one of those beautiful women we dined with last night?"

"I am a bachelor by choice," the Frenchman told her. "That is why, beautiful lady, I can concentrate on you without any woman trying to prevent me from doing so."

Salvia laughed.

"I will not find it difficult to concentrate when I am sailing home in his Lordship's yacht which is, I may say, one of the most comfortable yachts that I have ever seen anywhere."

She managed to change the conversation away from herself, but Monsieur Girard merely persisted,

"I would like to see you bathing in the sea. I am sure that your body must be as beautiful as your face."

As he was speaking to her in French, she thought that it sounded better than if it had been in English.

At the same time it was too intimate for her to feel anything but to be embarrassed by him.

She was thankful when the food arrived.

Salvia was not surprised when they ate a large and, she was sure, very expensive meal.

And they drank a great deal of excellent French wine.

She tried to talk of any subjects that he would know the answers to.

But he invariably brought the conversation back to her and her looks.

"If everyone admired me as much as you say you do," she said, "I should be enjoying myself in England, but as you well know the English gentlemen find it difficult to pay women elaborate compliments and prefer talking about their game shooting or their thoroughbred horses."

Monsieur Girard laughed.

"The Englishman does not understand *l'amour* as we French do, and that, my beautiful lady, is what I want to talk to you about."

"And I, being English, feel that we have not known each other long enough," Salvia replied stiffly.

She looked round the restaurant before she went on,

"Perhaps in a month or so I might well accept your compliments and be prepared to talk to you about love, but then we have only just met and I would feel embarrassed at discussing personal matters with someone I hardly know."

"That is all the more reason why you should know me better," he insisted.

She thought with amusement that he had an answer to everything that she might say.

In fact the way they talked over dinner might easily have been put on the stage and it would have been found amusing by the audience, even if they were English and not French.

They had four courses and were considering what fruit they should choose from quite a large selection, when, glancing at the clock, Salvia exclaimed,

"It is now getting late and I must go home or rather back to the hotel."

The Frenchman smiled.

"I have something very French to show you before that. It is a place that I am sure you will find amusing and very different from anything you will ever see in England."

Because he was so determined for her to do what he wanted, although she protested and said that she was tired, he whisked her away from the restaurant.

They went to a night club that fortunately was not far away.

It was obviously a smart place to go to because the other customers were all well dressed and the men were in evening clothes.

At the same time Salvia thought that it was not the sort of place she would be expected, as an unmarried girl, to visit.

But then she had to admit that the Monsieur Girard danced well.

The lights were lowered as they did so.

She felt that he held her too close and was anxious to leave long before he agreed to do so.

"You need not worry yourself about his Lordship getting back," the Frenchman said, "if that is in your mind. Dinner with the Emperor always means a huge amount of talking."

He paused before he added with a smile,

"Then if it is an all male party, he usually invites the most enchanting *courtesans* in Paris to amuse them afterwards."

Salvia looked at him in surprise.

"Surely this is a more serious occasion than if His Excellency was just entertaining his special friends."

"Beautiful women are essential to His Excellency," he replied. "Therefore, his Lordship will not be home until dawn."

He spoke so positively that Salvia thought it would be a mistake to argue with him.

She therefore danced with him again until she felt that he was being far too familiar and it was essential that she should somehow return to the hotel.

Salvia told Monsieur Girard that she was tired.

"I really have no wish to dance anymore," she said firmly.

He paid the bill for their dinner.

Then they drove back in his carriage.

When she reached the hotel, she realised that it was not particularly late in the evening and maybe she had been rather rude.

She therefore did not over-protest when he insisted on going up to her sitting room to have, as he said, 'a last drink.'

Lord Carville had left a bottle of white wine on the sideboard.

She poured Monsieur Girard out a glass and then said,

"Now you must let me retire to bed, as I have told you I am feeling very tired."

He took the wine glass from her hand and put it down.

Then he said,

"That is exactly what I am thinking we should do."

Almost before she realised what was happening, he pushed her through the door beside them.

It was open and so he realised that it led into her bedroom.

Although she struggled with him, he managed, as he was so strong, to throw her down onto the bed.

She had taken off her cape when she had come into the sitting room.

Now, as she struggled to sit up, she realised that he had taken off his coat.

Then he flung himself on top of her.

He was large for a Frenchman and she was helpless against him.

As he started to pull her dress off her shoulders, she screamed out.

"Let me go! *Let me go!*"

"I have been waiting for this all evening," he said in French.

Then, as she twisted her face so that he should not kiss her and shouted out again, a voice from the doorway exclaimed,

"What the devil is going on here?"

It was Lord Carville.

Salvia gave a murmur of delight

Lord Carville came up to the bed and then pulled the Frenchman up by his collar and dragged him roughly to his feet.

Without saying a word, he pushed him out of the bedroom and into the sitting room.

Salvia then heard the Frenchman give a shout and thought that Lord Carville must have hit him.

As she sat up on the bed and tried to pull her gown onto her shoulder, she heard the door slam.

A short moment later Lord Carville came hurrying into her bedroom.

"How could you have brought that man back here?" he asked harshly.

Salvia put her hands, which were both trembling, together as she replied,

"I did not mean to – but he insisted on having – a drink. Then he pushed me – in here."

"Surely you would know better," Lord Carville said angrily, "than to invite a Frenchman into your room when you are alone."

"He insisted on – coming," Salvia replied weakly.

She put her fingers up to her eyes.

"I did not – want to have dinner – with him, but he insisted because our hostess from last night was unable – to invite me to her house."

Lord Carville sat down on the bed beside her and put his arm round her.

"You have had a shock," he said quietly. "But you must have known that any Frenchman will always behave like this with a pretty woman."

"I did not want to go out with him," Salvia replied, "but I felt it was rude – not to go."

"This is something that you must never do again," Lord Carville asserted.

"I did not want to," Salvia said. "I did not think he would behave like that. It all happened – so quickly."

She was very near to tears.

He put his fingers under her chin and turned her face up to look at him.

"It's all right. It will never happen again because I will not let it. What we must do, darling, is to get married at once. Then no one will dare touch you ever again except for me."

She stared at him as she exclaimed,

"Married!"

"I love you, Salvia, as I have never loved anyone before and I just know that I cannot live without you. So the sooner we are married the happier and more content I will be."

Salvia did not speak and he went on,

"I will look after you, I promise, so that no man will ever make you unhappy again."

For a moment Salvia was absolutely breathless.

Then she stammered almost in a whisper,

"But – you don't know anything about me. You have no idea – who I am."

"I love you," Lord Carville replied. "I am in love with you more every day and every minute since we have been together. Now I must look after you or else I will lose you and that is something which must never ever happen."

He pulled her a little closer to him.

Then his lips were on hers.

She knew, as he kissed her, that her heart and her soul loved him as she had never loved anyone before.

# **CHAPTER SEVEN**

Lord Carville kissed Salvia and went on kissing her until she was limp in his arms.

She could scarcely believe that this was happening to her.

'I love you! I love you!' she wanted to shout out.

But she could only say it in her mind because her lips were being held completely captive.

Then at last as if he suddenly realised that he must look after her, he rose from the bed where he was sitting and laid her head very gently against the pillows.

"You must now go to sleep, my darling," he said. "Tomorrow we will make plans as to how soon we can be married. In fact we could be married here in Paris before we leave or we could ask the Captain of my yacht to marry us."

Salvia looked at him.

She felt as if she could no longer think of anything except that she loved him with all her heart.

His kiss was just as she had always thought a kiss should be.

No one before had ever kissed her on the lips.

She had always imagined in her dreams that a kiss was something almost holy and that was exactly what it had been for her.

'I love him! I love him!' she tried to murmur, but was incapable of bringing the words to her lips.

Almost as if he understood, Lord Carville looked down at her.

His eyes were very soft.

"You are so incredibly sweet," he said, "so utterly and completely wonderful. I must look after you because I could not bear to lose you. I would die rather than do so."

Then, just as if he did not trust himself, he walked towards the door.

"Get into bed, my precious," he turned to say, "and tomorrow we will make plans. At the moment, because I love you with all my heart and soul, it is impossible for me to think clearly."

Then, as if he forced himself to do so, he walked out through the door closing it quietly behind him.

For a moment Salvia could not move.

She felt as if it was all part of an astounding dream.

That what she was feeling was not at all real, but very different from anything she had felt or experienced before.

'This is love,' she mused. 'The love I have sought and the love I want to keep burning for the rest of my life and beyond.'

She did not move because she was deep in thought.

She told herself that the love Lord Carville had for her was totally different from what she thought love would be like.

She had not expected it to be so overwhelming.

When the men who she had danced with paid her compliments and then told her that they loved her, she had thought if that was love it was not as exciting as she had expected it to be.

Now she was sure that it was not only wonderful and beautiful it was so powerful.

She felt as if she was no longer herself and it was impossible to think.

'I love him! I love him!' she told herself over and over again.

Salvia had known that her love had been growing within her ever since they had been together.

Finally and with difficulty she forced herself to get ready for bed.

She took off her clothes, put on her nightgown and climbed into bed.

She pulled the bedclothes over her as if they were a protection.

She felt that, if her father knew what had happened here tonight, he would smile and tell her that Lord Carville was exactly the son-in-law he had wanted and the man he would have liked her to marry.

'He loves me for myself,' Salvia reflected.

This was very different from the other young men who had pursued her in London.

She had been certain that they had all been vividly conscious of her father's position in the Social world and that she herself was an asset that any man would want to acquire as a wife.

But Lord Carville was different.

He loved her even though he believed her to be nothing more than his secretary.

A woman who had to earn money to keep herself from starving.

'He loves me, he really loves me,' she whispered to herself almost in disbelief.

Then she closed her eyes and tried very hard to go to sleep.

It did not happen for some time.

But, because she had had such a tiring day and she had been so frightened when that dreadful Frenchman had flung himself upon her, she fell asleep.

\*

When she awoke, she realised that it was morning and the sun was now streaming in between the curtains.

For a long moment she thought that she must have dreamt what had happened last night.

Yet every nerve in her body told her that it was real and that Lord Carville would be waiting for her.

She jumped out of bed to wash and dress herself quickly.

'If he wants to get away,' she thought, 'I must not delay him in case he is caught again by the French wanting him to help them or wishing to make more fuss of him than they have already.'

When she looked in the mirror to see if her hair was tidy, she was surprised by her own face.

Her eyes were shining and she thought, although it seemed conceited, that she had never looked so pretty.

'I am in love – and he loves me,' she then told her reflection.

She hurried across the room and opened the door into the sitting room.

Breakfast was laid on the table.

For a moment she felt her heart throb because he was not there.

Even as she thought perhaps that she had lost him, the door opened and he came in.

For a moment they just gazed at each other.

Then he asked her,

"Did you sleep well, my darling? I lay awake most of the night thinking about you and I so wanted you in my arms."

"I – thought," Salvia answered almost in a whisper, "that it was perhaps – just a dream."

Lord Carville smiled.

"If it is a dream, it is one we must have again and again. You are now looking even more enchanting than I remember you to be."

Salvia blushed a little shyly and walked towards the breakfast table.

"How soon are we leaving for home?" she asked.

"As soon as you have had your breakfast and I have already asked my valet, who is packing my clothes, to help you with yours."

Salvia murmured her thanks and then she poured out his coffee.

He took it from her and asked as he did so,

"How is it at all possible that anyone could look as lovely as you do so early in the day? I have been thinking of you all night and I have never in my life seen anyone as glorious as you are."

Salvia blushed and replied,

"Now you are making me feel shy."

"I just adore you when you are shy," Lord Carville replied.

Then, as if he felt that they must hurry, he helped himself to a large dish of eggs and bacon and put his plate in front of him.

Salvia tried to eat something, but somehow it was just impossible.

Instead she drank a cup of coffee and waited, as she told herself, for his orders.

Then Lord Carville said,

"You have not yet told me, my darling, where you want to be married."

"Are you absolutely certain," Salvia asked him after a moment's pause, "that you really want to marry me? You said you did last night, but perhaps it would be unwise to do anything at all hasty until you have thought it over carefully. Otherwise you might well regret what you have done."

Lord Carville smiled.

"Do you really think," he questioned, "that at my age having been pursued for years, because I am of some social consequence, that I don't know who I love and who loves me?"

He put out his hands as he spoke and she put hers into them.

"I love you more than I could ever put into words," he said. "All I want is to make sure that I can look after and protect you for the rest of our lives together."

"It is marvellous you can say that," Salvia replied. "But I cannot tell you where I want to marry you before you meet my mother. She would be very hurt and think it very strange and unkind of me if I married someone she had never met and secretly, as it were, behind her back."

Lord Carville smiled.

"In which case we will hurry to England as quickly as we can. When I have met your mother, I will tell her that we love each other and I cannot believe that she will not welcome me as her son-in-law."

As she was touched at him being so understanding, Salvia looked at him and tried to find words to express just what she was feeling.

He merely bent his head and kissed her hand.

"I am in a hurry to get back to London," he said. "I don't think I have to tell you again the reason why."

He pulled Salvia to her feet and carried on,

"I feel sure that the packing must be finished by now. Let's hurry to the Station and back to the yacht."

"Are you quite sure," she asked, "that the French do not want you anymore?"

"If they do they will have to want," Lord Carville replied. "I want you and I cannot wait one minute longer than I have to before you are my wife."

They were standing closely beside each other as he spoke.

Then, as if she knew that he was about to kiss her and it was what she wanted more than anything with her heart and soul, Salvia ran to the communicating door into her bedroom.

She found, as she had expected, that his Lordship's valet had just finished packing her clothes.

Her coat and hat were lying on a chair waiting for her to put them on.

"Thank you, James," she said. "I am so glad that you have packed everything because his Lordship wants to leave immediately."

James smiled.

"His Lordship's always in a big hurry one way or another," he replied. "But I can understand him wantin' to get home. If you were to ask me he's had enough of them Froggies."

Salvia chuckled.

Then, putting on her hat and coat, she picked up her handbag.

As she did so, James carried her cases downstairs and through the door into the passage.

Salvia heard him speaking with Lord Carville, who must have come from his own room.

Salvia looked round the bedroom to see if anything had been left behind.

When she looked at the bed where she had been so frightened when Monsieur Girard had thrown himself on top of her, she gave a shiver.

Then she remembered how Lord Carville had taken her up to Heaven when he had kissed her.

So she would always remember this particular room and what it meant to her.

'He loves me! He loves me!' she told herself very happily.

She thought it almost too fantastic for words.

Then she realised that Lord Carville had come into the bedroom and was standing just behind her.

"Are you ready?" he asked. "James has taken our luggage downstairs."

"Yes, I know. I don't think that I have left anything behind."

Her voice grew a little unsteady.

She was still thinking of how much the kisses Lord Carville had given her last night still seemed to touch her lips as if it was impossible for her to forget them.

"If you look at me like that," he said unexpectedly, "I will kiss you again as I have kissed you last night and we might miss the train that is carrying us to Marseilles."

"You are quite right, we must go at once," Salvia agreed, turning towards the door.

But Lord Carville seized her hand and pulled her back to him.

"I want to kiss you more than I have ever wanted to do anything in my whole life," he murmured. "But because we are in a hurry I am trying to control myself."

She knew that she was longing for his kisses more than she could say in words.

But she recognised as he had said that they must hurry rather than miss the train.

She turned towards the door holding his hand and then together they almost ran to the top of the stairs and down them.

A carriage was waiting for them outside.

As it was a lovely sunny day, the hood was down and they could see and be seen as the horses drawing the carriage set off for the Railway Station.

They did not speak very much on the way.

But Salvia knew that every breath in her body was speaking of her love for him.

She felt that Lord Carville was thinking the same as her.

'I love him! I adore him!' she said to herself, 'how could I have been so fortunate as to find a man who loves me for myself and not because my father was so important or that we owned one of the most admired stately houses in London?'

She was certain that the men who had admired her at the parties she had enjoyed before her father died were thinking that if they wanted an important wife, it would be difficult to find one better suited than she was.

Everyone in the country respected her father and everyone thought that her mother was charming.

Her background was perfect from a social point of view.

'He loves me entirely for myself,' Salvia reflected. 'How could I ask for anything more sublime than that?'

The train was duly waiting for them at the Railway Station.

Salvia thought, as they climbed into it, that it was a good thing that no one they had been associated with since they had come to Paris was aware that Lord Carville was now leaving.

If they had, there would undoubtedly have been a number of people saying 'goodbye' to him.

Although it was unpleasant even to think of it, one or two of those who were chosen to look after the visitors to the Conference might have thought that it was their duty to accompany them to Marseilles.

As it was they each had their own compartment on the train

When they sat down in the one which Lord Carville had allotted to himself, they began to talk about all that had happened at the Conference.

They talked about how his speech, which had been so spectacular, would be remembered when perhaps what had been said by the other speakers would be forgotten.

"You were so splendid," Salvia told him. "No one who listened to you will ever forget what you said or the roar of applause that you received when you had finished."

"I have forgotten it already," he replied to her. "I am thinking about *you* and only you. It is impossible for me to believe that anything else in the whole world is of any significance whatsoever."

Salvia smiled.

"I don't believe I am hearing this, but if it is true, then I want to clap my hands for ages because you are so eloquent."

"I find it much easier to kiss you than to put it into words," Lord Carville sighed.

Salvia put up her hands and then moved a little way away from him.

"We must behave properly until we reach London," she insisted. "I am begging you not to make me travel too fast into a world I know nothing about."

"What do you mean by that?" Lord Carville asked.

Salvia did not look at him as she answered a little shyly,

"I had never been kissed before and it made me feel so strange and mysterious that I am almost afraid of you."

Lord Carville put out his hand and laid it on hers.

"Is that the truth," he enquired gently. "Has no one ever kissed you before?"

"Not a real kiss," Salvia replied.

"What do you feel about it?" he asked.

There was silence for a moment.

Then she said in a whisper,

"I thought that it was the most wonderful thing that had ever happened to me."

"I felt the same," he agreed. "But you are so right, my darling, we must keep our kisses until we are married. Only be kind to me and remember that it is agonising for me to behave as you want me to behave."

He sounded a little passionate as he added,

"I want to hold you close and tell you over and over again how much you mean to me."

"How is it possible that this had happened?" Salvia asked. "It is something I will always want to remember."

"There is a lot more I have to say," Lord Carville replied, "a lot more to make absolutely sure that you are really mine."

Salvia blushed and looked away as she said,

"Perhaps you will find me ignorant and therefore very different from the French ladies who pursued you so relentlessly."

Lord Carville laughed.

"So, you noticed that. I thought perhaps you might and I was not at all certain whether you would be shocked or jealous."

"I was not really shocked. It is just what I expected from the French. But I do believe that it means very little compared to what we are feeling now."

"I like the 'we'," Lord Carville said. "I have been so afraid that, if I said too much too quickly, that I might scare you."

He gave a sigh before he went on,

"You cannot imagine just how difficult it has been for me not to kiss you almost as soon as we stepped onto my yacht and I had you to all to myself."

"I had no idea – you were feeling like that," Salvia murmured.

"I realised that and it made me behave myself well, although I wanted, every night we were at sea, to come into your cabin and kiss you goodnight," he answered.

"I should have been surprised if you had done that," Salvia said, "and I expect rather shocked."

Lord Carville drew in his breath.

"I adore you," he told her, "I adore you and love you and I want to kiss you and go on kissing you. But it is something special that I do know I must keep until we are man and wife."

Because of the intensity in his voice, Salvia blushed and looked away.

"You promised to protect me," she said very softly. "I think perhaps you should also protect me from myself!"

"That is exactly what I am trying to do and I don't mind telling you that it is exceedingly difficult and almost agonising. In fact, because I don't want to shock you, I am going to walk up and down the corridor and look out of the open window and try to think of anything except you!"

Salvia gave a little laugh.

"I want you to think about me," she said. "But I know that you are right and, if when you get to London you change your mind and decide you will marry someone far more important than me, I will understand."

"There is no one in the world more important to me than you. I have been feeling like this ever since I first met you. You have to admit that I am very good at controlling myself, if nothing else."

"Did you really fall in love with me as soon as you saw me?" Salvia asked him shyly.

"I thought when we met there was something about you which made me believe that you were different from anyone I had ever met before," Lord Carville explained.

He hesitated for a moment before he went on,

"Then, when we worked together, I found myself watching the clock until you arrived in the morning and then feeling utterly lonely and abandoned when you left."

"I had no idea you felt like that."

"It was not particularly nice for me," Lord Carville answered. "But I told myself I was being ridiculous. That there were dozens of girls who, if I went to a dance, would welcome me eagerly and I would be very much approved of by their relations."

There was silence for a moment.

Then Salvia asked him,

"Suppose your relations are very angry because you have married me?"

"My relations, such as they are and indeed there are not that many of them, will do just as they are told and will welcome my bride with open arms."

Salvia did not speak and he continued,

"If you think I am good at directing the French how to behave, I can assure you that I am even better when it comes to making my family do exactly what I want them to do."

Then he added,

"Fortunately, as I have told you, there are not many of them and the majority are married with families, which keep them busy and prevent them from interfering in any way with me."

"So you think," Salvia replied softly, "they will not welcome me, believing that I am just not good enough for you?"

"They will think what I want them to think," Lord Carville said rather sharply. "That is that I am marrying the most perfect, the most wonderful and the most adorable woman in the whole wide world."

He laughed before he went on,

"I can assure you that they are far too frightened of me to criticise in any way what I do or, as they will now learn, who I want to marry."

Then as if he was not prepared to say anymore, he stood up and went out to the corridor and disappeared from sight.

'I love him! I love him!' she said to herself, 'and he loves me because I am me. I am quite certain that Papa is pleased that I have found the right man and I know that we will love each other not only now but much, much more as the years pass by.'

She drew in her breath and felt that her father was hearing every word that she was saying to herself.

'I love him, Papa, I love him,' she murmured to herself. 'I know if you were here you would welcome him as your son-in-law and be very pleased that he is so clever and so perfect in every way.'

When they arrived at Marseilles, it was to find the yacht looking spick and span.

The Captain was delighted to see them again and welcomed them by saying,

"I do hope, my Lord, that you are not returning immediately to England as we have all been hoping that you would be making one of your long journeys abroad."

He paused before he continued,

"I and the crew have bet on Egypt which, if you remember, we saw very little of on our last trip."

"I recall that very well, and I promise to go back," Lord Carville replied. "But first I have one very important engagement in England."

He laughed as he added,

"Then, as it is such good weather and the yacht is even smarter than I expected it to be, I promise you that we will visit Egypt and many other places as well."

"So your Lordship wishes to go back to England now," the Captain said in a slightly flat voice.

"I have to," Lord Carville told him. "But only for a short time, in fact time to make the yacht even smarter than it looks at the moment."

"That would be just impossible," Salvia intervened as she could see the disappointment on the Captain's face.

"I am teasing," Lord Carville admitted. "In fact I congratulate you, Captain, on making *The Seaspray* look so magnificent."

When he was alone with Salvia, he said,

"I am now planning our honeymoon, my darling. As you have never been to Egypt, it is somewhere I think you will enjoy. But first we will go to Greece."

Salvia gave a cry of joy.

"That is where I want to visit more than anywhere else in the world," she enthused. "I have read every book there is about Greece and I am quite certain that the Gods and Goddesses are waiting for us."

"I sensed that was what you were thinking," Lord Carville said. "I promise you, my glorious darling, that we will go to Mount Olympus and ask them to bless us and our love."

He smiled happily at her before he went on,

"When they do, it will be impossible for us ever to leave each other."

Salvia did not answer as she saw that he could read in her eyes how much she wanted to be in Greece with him.

"I love you," he sighed. "I love you more every moment of the day I am with you. We think the same and we feel the same. How is it possible that one can find so easily the other half of oneself."

"That is what the Greeks believe," Salvia replied, "which I thought completely impossible."

"But you do admit that you are the other half of me?" Lord Carville questioned.

"As long as you are content for me to be the other half of you," Salvia answered softly, "then I am very happy and honoured for you to be the other half of me."

"If you say things like that and look at me with those starlight eyes of yours, I will have to kiss you and go on kissing you until we reach England."

Salvia looked down shyly.

"You are not to tempt me," Lord Carville protested, "or make it impossible for me not to love you as I want to do and will do for ever once we are married."

He looked up at the sky overhead.

"Oh, why," he sighed deeply, "do I have to wait so long?"

"Now you are being unkind," Salvia pointed out.

"Why?" he asked.

"Because I love you as much as you love me, "and it is difficult for me to keep you waiting. But you know I am right in saying that my mother who loves me deeply, would be unbelievably hurt if I married you without her being present."

Lord Carville drew in his breath.

Then he said,

"There is no other answer that I can give to you, but, of course, I agree."

\*

They reached London in what seemed to be record time.

In fact the Captain was so pleased at the way they passed through the Bay of Biscay and so down the English Channel that he was sure, when he compared it with other Captains, he would undoubtedly be a winner.

They were, however, obliged to spend three hours on board before they moved into the River Thames later in the afternoon.

"We will be home in time for tea," Salvia said.

"You have not yet told me where your home is," Lord Carville commented.

"I want it to be a surprise. In fact I think I must warn you that there are several surprises waiting for you."

"Now you are trying to frighten me," Lord Carville complained. "But I will never be frightened of anything or anyone except you. I have no intention of losing you after all we have been through."

"I have no wish to lose you either," Salvia replied. "Don't forget I love you too."

They gazed at each other.

She just knew that Lord Carville was longing to kiss her.

She wanted his kisses, but she knew that they had both been wise in waiting as they had done on the train and on the yacht.

'I love him! I love him so much that I want to make certain that he loves me and me alone,' Salvia thought to herself last night. 'No other man would have been so kind and so understanding. No other man would have agreed to wait until he has met my mother and our engagement is approved by her.'

She felt as if her love for him was increasing day by day and hour by hour.

She felt sure that once they were married it would go on increasing as long as they lived.

'I love him! I adore him,' she said to herself over and over again.

If it was hard for him not to kiss her, it was hard for her not to want his kisses and to long for the torment she had made for both of them to be over.

At the same time she knew that she must behave as her mother would expect of her in the circumstances.

Most of their friends would be very shocked at the idea of her being alone on a yacht with such an attractive man.

They would imagine, feeling as they did, that they would have little or no control over themselves.

'He has proved his love for me and I know that he really does love me,' Salvia said to herself. 'I know now that love is the most powerful force in the Universe and I know too that love cannot fail.'

She only prayed that he would understand when he met her dear mother why they had to come back from the Mediterranean where they were to spend their honeymoon.

"There is so much I want to show you," he told her a dozen times a day.

They compared notes on the history of the different countries that they had visited.

They found after a short while that they could add to each other's knowledge in a way that made everything seem even more romantic and exciting than it would have done otherwise.

"Now you must tell the coachman where to take us," Lord Carville said when they left the yacht.

Their luggage had already been packed onto a hired carriage.

Salvia stepped into it and, when Lord Carville was beside her, she slipped her hand into his.

"We are now home!" she exclaimed. "And London looks just the same as it did before we left. I had a feeling because we had been through so much that it would look different."

Lord Carville laughed.

"I expect it is full of the same old scandal and the same parties. There will be the same people saying the same things as they did before we left."

"I am sure you are right," she agreed. "Therefore, I am hoping to give you something new to think about."

"I am most certainly looking forward to meeting your mother," Lord Carville told her.

Salvia had deliberately spoken in a low voice when she had told the coachman to drive to Wenlock House.

Lord Carville, who had been looking to see that the luggage was secure, had not heard her.

When they turned at Hyde Park Corner and drove into Park Lane, she saw that he looked rather surprised.

When they drove in past some impressive-looking gates and up to her home, she was aware that Lord Carville not only looked surprised but she felt his body stiffen.

It was then it occurred to her for the first time that he might suspect that her mother was perhaps earning her living by being a housekeeper or a cook to the influential people who lived in Wenlock House.

She said nothing.

When the carriage came to a standstill outside the front door, she turned to Lord Carville,

"Here we are and if later you want to go back to your own house, you had better keep this carriage to take you there."

Lord Carville did not answer.

Salvia stepped out.

As she did so, the front door was opened by the old butler.

"Here you are, my Lady," he said, "and about time too. Her Ladyship was getting ever so worried something might have happened to you."

"Where is my mother?" Salvia asked him.

"She's in the drawing room, my Lady," the butler replied, "and I know your Ladyship'll be glad to hear she's alone."

Without looking at Lord Carville to see the surprise in his eyes, Salvia ran towards the drawing room.

One of the footmen was holding open the door for her.

Her mother was sitting sedately on the sofa reading a newspaper.

She looked up in surprise as Salvia entered.

And then she gave a cry of delight.

"Darling, you are back!" she exclaimed. "I was just wondering when you would return."

"Yes, I am back, Mama. I could not let you know when we were leaving as we were not sure ourselves until the last moment."

She kissed her mother affectionately.

Then she turned round to see Lord Carville beside her looking, she thought, somewhat bemused.

"Mama, this is Lord Carville, who was a friend of Papa's and who, as you know, I have been with in France."

"You are a very naughty girl to have gone without telling me what you were doing," her mother scolded her.

Holding out her hand to Lord Carville, she said,

"I am delighted to meet you as my husband often spoke about you and told me how much he admired you."

"Of course, I knew your husband very well," Lord Carville replied. "If there was any admiring to do, it was I who admired him."

"I thought that Salvia would be safe working for you," the Countess said. "But I had no idea that she would have to go abroad."

"She was looked after very well. As you may have read in the newspapers the French were hosting a special Conference and I could not have managed if your daughter had not been with me."

"Now we have something very exciting to tell you, Mama," Salvia declared.

The Countess looked from Salvia to Lord Carville, who said,

"I believe that Salvia wants me to tell you that we love each other and we want to be married immediately. That is why she has insisted on coming here to tell you first and, of course, to ask for your blessing."

He spoke clearly and slowly.

Salvia could not help thinking that he had taken the shock of realising who she was with great dignity.

"You want to be married!" the Countess exclaimed. "Oh, darling, I know that your father would have been delighted. In fact I must tell you how pleased I am to meet his Lordship."

She turned to Lord Carville as she went on,

"I was very fond of your mother. We shared a Governess at one time and your father always stayed with us for our shoots in the country. I was enchanted by both of them."

"You can understand then why I am so anxious to marry your daughter. And how much my family will be so delighted at the idea."

Salvia thought as he spoke that he was playing his part very well.

She had seen astonishment in his eyes when they had entered the house and also when he saw her mother.

Now he said,

"I am hoping, Lady Wenlock, that you will allow your daughter to marry me as soon as possible."

"Well, of course, if that is what you want. I am so glad she has found someone my husband always admired who I know would be delighted to have you as a son-in-law."

Her mother was doing beautifully, Salvia thought, as she smiled and said,

"Darling Mama. I will have to buy my trousseau very quickly as Ivan wants to take me away on his yacht and you remember how I loved seeing other countries with Papa."

Then before Lady Wenlock could respond, Salvia asked,

"By the way, where are our guests?"

"It is excellent news. They have been asked to the country by some friends who are throwing a ball tomorrow night. They have insisted that they stay there for the Races so I am not expecting them back in London for at least a week."

Salvia clapped her hands.

"That is splendid and now we can have you all to ourselves. We can tell Ivan, who had no idea until now that you are my mother, exactly what we have been doing and how difficult everything has been for us."

"Not too difficult," the Countess replied, "thanks to you, my darling."

Even as she spoke, the door opened and the butler announced almost shouting the words,

"Lord and Lady Donald, my Lady."

Salvia turned round in amazement.

She saw her brother come into the room.

With him was a very pretty girl who looked almost too young to be grown up.

The Countess gave a cry of delight and hurried over the room to her son.

"Donald!" she cried. "You are back home! How marvellous."

"Yes, I am back," Donald said. "I have brought my wife with me who is longing to meet you. I know you will welcome her into our home."

If Lady Wenlock was astounded by his reply, she did not show it.

Instead, after kissing her son, she turned to the girl beside him.

"Are you really married to my son?" she asked her. "If so, I must tell you that I am certain you will be very happy."

"We are very happy," the girl answered. "And I am so excited to be here in England."

She had a very definite American accent.

"I am sure you are," the Countess said. "Now you must meet my daughter."

Salvia was at that moment kissing her brother.

Quietly, so that the others could not hear her, she questioned him,

"Is everything all right? Have you brought anything back?"

"Far more than I expected," Donald replied. "I have a great deal to tell you."

"I have a great deal to tell you too," Salvia said. "I am engaged to be married, but you have beaten me to the post!"

"I thought you would say that," he laughed. "But they would not allow me to bring her home unless we were married and I feel, at this moment, that we don't want a host of strangers imposing on us."

"You are quite right, Donald," Salvia agreed.

She drew her brother to one side while her mother was talking to her new daughter-in-law and said in a low whisper,

"I must tell you why I am here and that I am going to marry Lord Carville. I thought he should know who I am first of all and also meet Mama."

"How thrilling!" Donald exclaimed. "I thought that I was to be the hero of the family play, but I think you have stolen the main part!"

"I am not married yet, but you are," Salvia replied, "and I think she looks sweet."

"She just happens to be the only child of the richest man in the whole of America," her brother boasted. "At the same time I will make it clear that I love her very much and that she loves me."

Salvia gave a sigh of relief.

"But you obtained some of our money back from Walter?" she quizzed him.

"I got over half and he has promised to give the rest back, but really it does not matter now."

"I should think not," Salvia sighed.

She could hardly believe that what she had heard was true.

That her brother had really married a great heiress.

As she knew that an heiress in America was just the right word for the millions of dollars that Americans had made one way and another.

However, she was determined not to lose her own exciting dream just because her brother had turned up with one of his own.

She went back to where Lord Carville was standing by the fireplace and slipped her hand into his.

"There is so much excitement going on," she said. "So let's get married as soon as possible and get away from it all."

"Do you really mean that, my darling?" he asked.

"I want to be with you alone," Salvia answered.

"And God knows I want to be with you. Let's make it clear that if your mother wants a grand Wedding she has to arrange it with all possible speed. If not, you and I will get married tonight and run away at once as we have done before."

Salvia laughed.

"It sounds much too easy. So how am I to buy my trousseau?"

"I will buy you one in every country we visit," Lord Carville replied. "If you end up in nothing but a loin cloth, it will be your own fault!"

Salvia laughed again.

"I want to look lovely – for you," she murmured.

"You always look lovely and I want to hold you in my arms. A large ball dress would be in the way."

Salvia chuckled because she could not help it.

Then, as her mother came towards her, she said,

"With all this excitement going on, Ivan and I want to be married quickly. How soon, Mama, can you arrange a Wedding which is at least large and grand enough to be respectable."

She paused before she added,

"We don't want an enormous crowd of onlookers rather just our very close friends."

"I know just what you want," the Countess replied. "I think you could easily be married in under a week if you arrange the Church and bridesmaids if you intend to have them, while I arrange the Reception here in the ballroom and we must invite all your friends."

Salvia bent forward and kissed her mother.

"You are marvellous, Mama. Only you would take all this so calmly and not have hysterics yourself."

"I have no intention of having hysterics," she said firmly. "But I am very glad that Donald has married such a nice looking girl and I feel certain that she will make him very happy."

"She is the daughter of one of the richest man in America," Salvia whispered to her mother.

"Money does not always make happiness, but it at least saves us from having more people to stay here. The Meltons are charming, but I am looking forward to having the house to myself."

"Of course, you are," Salvia agreed. "If you will arrange for the Wedding Reception to take place here, then Ivan and I will organise the Service at the Church to take place as soon as possible."

"I was just thinking," her mother said, "that, as it is such lovely weather we could hold the Reception in the garden. The flowers will make a beautiful backdrop for the guests to admire."

"I think that is a very sensible idea," Salvia replied. "Of course, more people will want to be invited than we really want, but we will just have to make the best of it."

"I could not have you being married in some secret manner," her mother asserted. "People will be sure to say that you had got into trouble in one way or another."

She paused before she added,

"After all no one could make you a better husband than Ivan and your dear father had the greatest admiration for him."

"Just as I have and Mama, we are going to be as happy as you and Papa were."

"I hope that is true, darling," she replied. "Now I had better see what arrangements Donald is going to make for his wife and, of course, we are very lucky in that our American guests are staying away at least until the end of the week."

"Then we will be married before they return," Salvia said. "We don't want any strangers here, only our friends who will say and do the right thing."

Her mother laughed, but Salvia had already turned away to go to Lord Carville's side.

She slipped her hand into his and said,

"Mama says that she can have everything arranged for three days' time. It means that we have to stay up all night making a list of those who must be invited."

"Nonsense!" he exclaimed. "The last thing I want is too many people staring at me. All I want is to be alone with you, Salvia."

"As I want to be alone with you," Salvia whispered. "But everything has come right as I knew it would. I am sure that it is due to all my prayers and Papa is organising everything from Heaven."

"As long as he is organising you into my arms, I am content for him to do what he wishes. If I don't kiss you now, I think I will go mad!"

Lord Carville looked lovingly at her as he added,

"So show me the view from the top of the house or let's go to the cellar for a bottle of champagne. Either up or down as long as I can kiss you when we get there!"

Salvia laughed.

Taking him by his hand she then drew him out of the room and up the stairs.

When they arrived at the top floor, there was still another staircase to climb up to the top of the house from which there was a very good view of London.

However, Lord Carville had no desire to see any view at this moment.

He only wanted to look into Salvia's eyes and feel the softness of her lips.

When he closed the door, which led onto the roof, he took her into his arms.

He kissed her in the same way that he had kissed her before, as if he was drawing her heart from her body.

She knew, as he did so, that it was what he had been longing for all day.

She felt herself sinking rapidly into his arms until they seemed as if they were one person rather than two.

There was a comfortable sofa on the roof where the Countess often lay after luncheon instead of resting in her own bedroom.

Lord Carville sat down on it and pulled Silvia onto his knees.

"I love you! I adore you!" he breathed. "I predict, and I just know I am right, that we will be the happiest two people in the whole world once you are mine."

"I love you too, Ivan. Now there are no difficulties about us being married and I can tell you why I came to you because we needed the money, which has now been returned to us."

"It may seem a tragedy to you," Lord Carville said, "but it was certainly a joy and a wonder to me when you came to me as my secretary."

He pulled her a little closer as he murmured,

"Supposing I had never met you, supposing we had never found each other. But now we have, we are going to be very very happy. Everything in the future is going to be in a cloud of glory."

"That is just what I want for you because you are so clever," Salvia replied. "But you must not be so clever that you don't spend a great deal of your time with me."

"I am going to spend all of my time with you," he promised, "most specially on our honeymoon when we are going to explore a great deal of the world that you have not already seen."

He paused before he went on,

"Most of all you are going to explore me and love me with all my good points as well as my bad ones."

"I don't believe that you have any bad ones," Salvia replied. "I love you with my heart and my soul and I have nothing else to give you."

"That is all that I could ever desire," Lord Carville answered.

Then he was kissing her.

Kissing her until she felt as if they were both flying through the sky and into Heaven itself.

She knew that this was the love that she had always wanted and which she thought she would never find.

The love they had found with each other came from God, was part of God and was theirs for Eternity.

Printed in Great Britain
by Amazon